The Maze
of the Beast

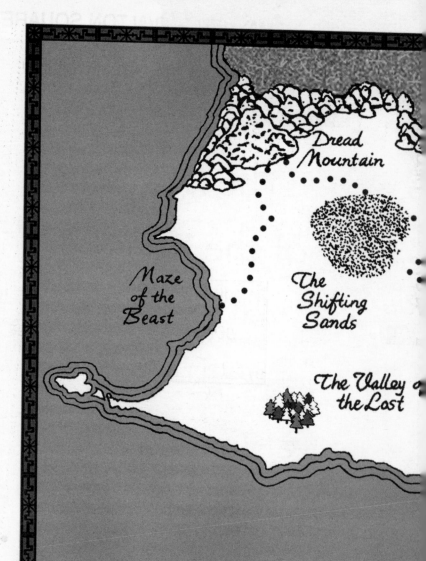

Dread
Mountain

Maze
of the
Beast

The
Shifting
Sands

The Valley o
the Lost

THE LAND OF

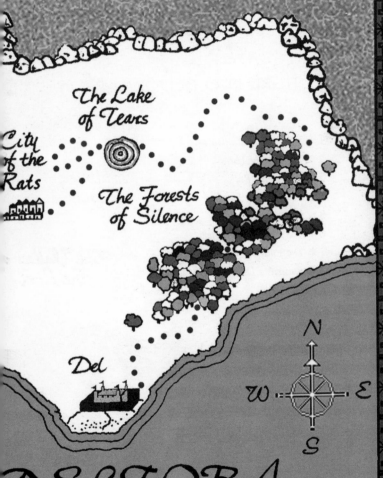

The Shadowlands

The Lake
of Tears

City
of the
Rats

The Forests
of Silence

Del

N
W   E
S

DELTORA

VENTURE INTO DELTORA

The Maze
of the Beast

EMILY RODDA

Scholastic Inc.

New York   Toronto   London   Auckland   Sydney
Mexico City   New Delhi   Hong Kong   Buenos Aires

ISBN 0-439-81699-8

12 11 10 9 8 7 6 5 4 3 2 1   6 7 8 9 10 11/0

Printed in the U.S.A.
First American continuity edition, January 2006

J.S.F.
ROD

b174446235

Contents

The story so far . . .

Sixteen-year-old Lief, fulfilling a pledge made by his father before he was born, is on a great quest to find the seven gems of the magic Belt of Deltora. The gems were stolen from the Belt to open the way for the evil Shadow Lord to invade Deltora. Hidden in fearsome places throughout the land, they must be restored to the Belt before the heir to the throne can be found and the Shadow Lord's tyranny ended.

Lief's companions are the man Barda, who was once a Palace guard, and Jasmine, a girl of Lief's own age who they met in the fearful Forests of Silence. On their travels the three have discovered a secret resistance movement led by Doom, a mysterious scar-faced man who rescued them when they were captured by the brutal Grey Guards.

Five gems have been found. The topaz, symbol of faith, has the power to contact the spirit world, and to clear the mind. The ruby, symbol of happiness, pales when danger threatens, repels evil spirits, and is an antidote to venom. The opal, gem of hope, gives glimpses of the future. The lapis lazuli, the heavenly stone, is a powerful talisman. The powers of the emerald, for honor, are still to be discovered.

Following the map Lief's father drew for him, the companions are now on their way to the coast and their next goal — The Maze of the Beast. Haste and secrecy are all-important, for the Shadow Lord has become aware of them, and Lief has learned that his parents have been imprisoned.

Now read on . . .

1 ~ Rescue

Lief, Barda, and Jasmine moved from Dread Mountain to the River Tor in silence and in haste, glad of the trees sheltering them from the open sky. For many days they had been travelling like this, all too aware that at any moment an enemy might strike. For many nights they had slept in turns, fully dressed, with their weapons in their hands.

Soon they would reach the river. They knew they had only to follow it to reach Deltora's west coast. There, somewhere, was the next goal marked on their map — the horribly named Maze of the Beast. There, if Lief's father was right, lay the sixth stone of the Belt of Deltora.

But the Shadow Lord's servants were watching for them — waiting for them to show themselves. The Shadow Lord knew that the topaz had been taken from the Forests of Silence, that the ruby was gone

1

from the Lake of Tears, and the opal from the City of the Rats. Perhaps by now he even suspected that the lapis lazuli had in its turn been wrested from its terrible guardian in the Shifting Sands.

If the Dread Gnomes were successful in deceiving him, it would be some time before he realized that the emerald had already gone the way of the other four gems. But his servants would be in this area by now, lurking in the mountain's foothills or searching from its skies. And the Maze of the Beast, and every road to it, would be guarded well by enemies searching for the group that fitted the description they had been given: a man, a boy, and a wild girl with a black bird.

Lief looked ahead at Kree, hunched gloomily on Jasmine's shoulder beside Filli. Poor Kree wanted to stretch his wings. But it was too dangerous for him to be seen too much in the air, in case his presence marked their position for an enemy. So he was forced to stay close to the ground, and he did not like it.

None of us like it, thought Lief. It is unpleasant to scurry like hunted creatures through this rustling forest. Unpleasant to fear the coming of night. But there is no help for it.

He jumped as Jasmine abruptly swung to one side, snatching her dagger from her belt. Kree fluttered into the air, squawking. Lief caught a glimpse of bright, dark eyes and a pointed snout in the bushes. Then there was the scuffle of tiny, escaping paws and the next moment Jasmine was sheathing her weapon once more, snorting in disgust.

"I am jumping at shadows and fighting wood mice, now," she muttered, as she held out her arm to Kree and strode on down the rough pathway. "I cannot rid myself of the feeling that we are being watched."

"I have felt it for days," Barda answered, glancing back at her. "The forest seems full of eyes."

Lief said nothing. He was very conscious of the Belt clasped around his waist. He felt that the hidden watchers must be aware of it, though it was concealed under his shirt, with his jacket buttoned closely over the top. It was far heavier than it had been when first he put it on, empty, in Del. The power and magic of the gems that now studded five of its medallions seemed to weigh it down.

Suddenly there was a faint, shrill cry and a splash from somewhere ahead. The companions stopped dead. The splashing grew louder and more desperate. At a word from Jasmine, Kree took wing and flew towards the sound.

"Marie! Marie!" screamed a high-pitched voice. "Oh, Marie . . ."

"What is it?" Lief breathed. "Barda, quickly! It sounds as if — "

"We must take care," Barda warned. "It could be a trick. Wait — "

But already Kree was flying back towards them, screeching urgently.

"Someone is in the water!" exclaimed Jasmine. "Someone is drowning!"

They began to run, their feet pounding on the narrow path, the sound of the despairing voice growing louder and more shrill by the moment, the sound of splashing growing less and less.

They burst through the last of the trees onto a broad bank of fine white sand. The river stretched, glittering, before them, deep and swiftly running. A young girl, no more than five or six years old, was drifting in the shallows, clinging to the floating branch of a tree. It was she who was screaming, vainly holding out her hand to another child who was struggling in deeper water, beside an overturned raft.

In moments, Lief and Barda had cast aside their boots and swords and were wading into the water. "You get the one nearest the shore," Barda shouted over his shoulder to Lief as he struck out for the raft. "Make haste, Lief, or we will lose her. The river is running fast."

Lief waded to the child holding the branch and managed to catch her before she was swept out of reach. She clutched at him frantically as he lifted her up and into his arms. She was deathly cold. The water lapped around his chest as he struggled back towards the shore.

"Marie!" the girl sobbed, shuddering and straining to look back at the overturned raft. "I fell in and she tried to help me and then she fell in, too! I caught

4

hold of the branch, but she . . . Oh, where is she? Where is she?"

Lief looked around and his heart sank. Barda had almost reached the raft, but where Marie had been there was only swirling water.

Barda took a deep breath and dived. In moments he had appeared again, dragging a limp, white bundle. He began swimming back to shore, paddling with one arm, dragging the bundle after him with the other.

"She is drowned!" screamed the child.

"No. She was not under for long. She will be all right," Lief said, more confidently than he felt. He waded on, feeling with relief the water growing shallower as he climbed up to the bank where Jasmine was waiting with a blanket.

"I will see to her. Help Barda!" Jasmine said crisply, wrapping the blanket around the little girl.

"I am Jasmine," Lief heard her say as he ran to where Barda was splashing to shore, clutching his limp, sodden burden. "This is Filli, and Kree. What is your name?"

"Ida," cried the child. "I am Ida. Oh, take me away from the river! I do not wish to see it anymore! Marie is drowned. She is drowned!"

Lief plunged once again into the water and helped Barda carry the unconscious child up onto the bank. Like Ida, she was chilled to the bone. They laid her down gently. As he saw her face, Lief gasped in surprise. Straight brown hair, fine golden skin, heart-shaped face, long, curling black eyelashes — why, she looked exactly like Ida, even to the small brown mark on the left cheekbone, and the simple white dress. They were twins! Identical in every detail.

What were twin girls, so young, too, doing in this wilderness alone? Where were their parents?

Barda had turned Marie on her side and was bending over her, his face grim.

"Is she dead?" Lief whispered. Somehow the thought was even more terrible now that he knew the girls were twins. It was dreadful to think of one of them being left alone. He glanced up and was relieved to see that Jasmine was beginning to lead the sobbing Ida off the riverbank, towards the trees.

Then, as Jasmine stepped aside to let the little girl move onto the path before her, Lief saw a tiny movement in the undergrowth nearby. Before he could move or cry a warning, there was a twang and an arrow was flying through the air.

It struck Ida in the back. She crumpled and fell forward without a cry. With a shout of outrage, Lief leaped for her attacker. His sword was lying out of reach. He did not care. He was angry and shocked enough to deal with this bare-handed.

He tore the concealing bushes aside and threw himself on the dark-haired boy who crouched there. Knocking the deadly bow from the boy's hand, he hurled him out on the sand. The killer fell heavily on his face, his arm crumpled under him, and lay still, moaning in pain. Lief ran for his sword, snatched it up. His ears were roaring. There was murder in his heart as he spun around once more.

Groaning, the boy on the ground rolled onto his back. He tried to rise, and fell back again, grimacing and holding his arm.

"Do you not see — they are Ols! Ols!" he shouted.

Then Lief heard Barda's gurgling shout, heard Jasmine's scream. He looked up.

Ida's body had disappeared. And Marie, little Marie, was rising from the sand. She had Barda by the throat, her white fingers digging deep into his flesh. Her teeth were bared. And then her body was bubbling, stretching, growing till it was a tall, wavering white shadow with a black mark at its center and an enormous peaked head like a ghastly bleached candle flame. The thing's eyes were burning red and the mouth was a toothless black hole, but it laughed like a child as Barda staggered back and fell beneath its weight.

2 ~ Fate Takes a Hand

Gasping in horror, Jasmine and Lief both lunged forward, stabbing and tearing at the thing, trying to pull it away from Barda. The cold, wavering mass shrank and re-formed. The thing staggered, but its grip held.

"Through the heart!" the injured boy shouted. "Stab it through the heart! Kill it outright or it will finish him!"

"It is stabbed through the heart already," Jasmine shrieked. "It does not fall."

Growling, the thing turned on her. With a cry she was swept aside by a rush of white that sent her sprawling.

"Now, Lief! Strike on the right side!" the boy screamed. "The heart is on the right side, not the left!"

Lief plunged his sword home. The thing shuddered, then collapsed, its body a shapeless, writhing mass bulging horribly here and there with limbs, faces, claws, ears. Choking with disgusted horror, Lief recognized the face of Marie, the pointed snout of a wood mouse, the wing of a bird . . .

Then there was just a bubbling pool of white, that sank, as he watched, into the sand.

Barda lay shivering and coughing, the breath rasping in his throat. Already the dark red marks of the Ol's strangling fingers on his neck were darkening to purple. But he was alive.

"He was lucky. Another minute and it would have been too late."

Lief spun around and saw that the boy he had attacked had managed to crawl to his feet and was standing behind him. He heard Jasmine exclaim and glanced at her. She was staring at the boy in amazement.

"It is you!" she exclaimed. "The boy who served the drinks at the Rithmere Games. You are one of Doom's band. You are Dain."

The boy nodded briefly, then limped to where Barda was lying and looked down at him. "Your friend needs warming," he said. "He is wet, and Ol attacks chill to the bone."

He turned away and began walking slowly towards the trees.

Lief hastened to make a fire and heat water for tea while Jasmine ran for more blankets. By the time Dain returned, dragging a small backpack, his injured arm in a rough sling, Barda was well wrapped up and sitting close to a crackling blaze. The terrible shivering had eased and the color had begun to return to his face.

"Thank you," he said to Dain huskily. "If it had not been for you . . ." He winced, and lifted a hand to his throat.

"Do not try to speak," Dain advised. He turned to Lief, holding out a jar he held in his uninjured hand. "A warm drink sweetened with this will help him," he said. "It strengthens, and eases pain. It is very powerful. One spoonful should be enough."

The jar bore a small handmade label.

Lief unscrewed the lid and sniffed at the jar's golden contents, drawing in the sweet scent of apple blossom. "Quality Brand," he murmured, glancing at Dain. "The initials are interesting, but the name itself is ordinary. So ordinary, in fact, that I suspect it is false."

"As false as the names you gave at the Rithmere Games, Lief," the boy answered evenly. "These are hard times. You are not the only ones who must be careful."

Lief nodded, realizing that he had overheard them calling to one another before the Ols' attack. There was no help for it, but it was unfortunate.

He took a mug of tea and stirred a small amount of the honey into the steaming brew. Then he gave the mug to Barda, who wrapped both hands around its warmth and sipped gratefully.

"What are these Ols?" Jasmine demanded, as she passed Dain a mug of tea for himself.

"Shape-changers from the Shadowlands," Dain said, stirring a spoonful of honey into his own cup. "The Shadow Lord uses them to do his evil work. Perhaps I should not be surprised that you have not heard of them before. They are more common here, in the west, than in the east, where you come from."

He paused, watching them under his brows. Barda, Lief, and Jasmine remained expressionless. Did he think they were going to fall into so simple a trap?

Dain laughed easily and bent to draw in the sand.

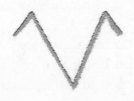

The mark of the Resistance. The companions looked at it in silence, then glanced at one another.

Dain leaned forward. "We are both on the same side, are we not?" he asked earnestly, suddenly dropping his easygoing manner. "What does it matter if I know where you live? Doom says — "

"How did you come to be here?" Jasmine asked abruptly. "How did you find us?"

Dain drew back, and his face closed once more. "I was not looking for you. I was returning to our western stronghold when I saw the Ols. I knew them for what they were. Grade One Ols are crude and cannot hold a form for very long. They are easy to recognize when you know what to look for. I followed them, waiting my chance to destroy them. And then, lo and behold, you appeared, and the Ols were plainly interested."

He paused. "They have been following you for days, you know," he added in a hard voice. "They took the shape of wood mice and watched your every move, listened to you, deciding how they would proceed. In the end, they chose to appeal to your tenderness of heart. Once they had separated you, they would have struck. You would have had no chance."

Lief, Jasmine, and Barda glanced at one another. All felt ashamed.

"We thank you for aiding us," Barda said stiffly at last. "We ask you to forgive our suspicion and secrecy. We have learned to be cautious."

"As have I," said Dain, still in that hard voice, "though for a moment I forgot myself in the pleasure of seeing familiar faces."

Lief suddenly realized that the boy was older than he had thought — at least as old as he was himself. The slight body, the fine-boned face, and the silkiness of the dark hair that flopped carelessly over Dain's forehead had deceived him.

Dain swallowed the last of his tea and stood up awkwardly, protecting his injured arm. "I will leave you in peace. Be on the watch for Ols. Grade Ones, like the two we have just dispatched, always travel in pairs. The others — well, you will probably not recognize them, anyway. It is best to trust no one."

He shouldered his pack and turned to go.

"Wait!" Lief exclaimed impulsively, jumping to his feet. "You cannot travel alone! Your arm is hurt. You cannot use your bow, or even a dagger."

"I will be all right," Dain said. "I do not have very far to go."

But Barda was shaking his head. "Wait one night, and we will escort you," he croaked, his hand on his throat. "It is the least we can do."

Lief saw Jasmine stiffen. Clearly, she did not approve of this plan. She does not want to see Doom again, he thought suddenly. She distrusts him. But Jasmine said nothing, and Dain seemed not to notice her expression.

He was hesitating. It was plain that his pride,

which urged him to leave them, was struggling with his common sense, which told him that it was madness to travel unprotected if he had a choice.

At last, he nodded. "Very well," he said, dropping his pack. "Thank you. I will wait. Then we will go together to the stronghold." He paused, biting his lip. "It is to the southeast. It is out of your way."

"How do you know? We have not told you where we are going," Jasmine snapped.

Dain's delicate face flushed red. "I thought perhaps that you may be travelling to — to Tora," he stammered.

Jasmine stared. The name meant nothing to her. But Lief was thinking furiously.

Tora! Del's great sister city in the west. He had been taught of it. But it was so long since he had heard its name that he had forgotten it existed!

Dain was waiting for an answer, leaning forward anxiously.

"Indeed," Barda said smoothly. "Well, if we are going to Tora, it will not hurt us to reach it a day or two later than we had planned."

Jasmine stood up. "I will find a secure place to camp for the night," she said. She stalked off into the trees, with Kree flying ahead. Dain gazed after her, and Lief saw a flicker of admiration in his eyes.

Lief felt an unsettling twinge of jealousy, bit his lip, and turned away. If only I had not injured him, he thought. Then he could have gone his way, and we could have gone ours.

Immediately he felt ashamed. He told himself that he was just upset because the journey to the Resistance stronghold would waste precious time. Every day of delay was another day his father and mother remained in danger, perhaps in torment, in the dungeons of the Shadow Lord in Del.

But, if he was honest, he also had to admit that he did not want Dain as a companion, even for a short time.

Dain made him uncomfortable. His gentle, polite ways were appealing, his quiet dignity was impressive, and, despite his lack of great strength, he had acted bravely in saving them from the Ols. But though he seemed easygoing on the surface, Lief could sense that there was something deep inside him that was hidden. Some secret he kept to himself.

No doubt he feels the same about us, Lief thought. And, of course, he is right. So we do not trust one another. That is the root of the problem. While we are with Dain we cannot discuss our quest, or the Belt. We cannot discuss my parents, or wonder aloud how they are faring. We cannot be comfortable.

Restless, unwilling to stay by the fire with Dain and Barda any longer, he went to help Jasmine. But as he walked into the trees, a new idea occurred to him.

Fate had played strange tricks on them before —

and somehow it had always turned out for the best. Could there be some reason for their being forced to keep Dain's company? Were they somehow *meant* to get to know him? Were they *meant* to go to the Resistance stronghold? To see Doom again?

Only time would tell.

3 - A Hard Journey

When they were settled under the overhanging tree Jasmine had found, Dain told them more about Ols. Listening to his soft, even voice, Lief began to feel that if they *had* been intended to spend time with him, this information alone may have been the reason.

"They are everywhere," Dain said, pulling his blanket more tightly around him. "They can take the shape of any living thing. They do not eat or drink, but Grade Twos can pretend to do so, just as they can create body heat to disguise what they are. In its natural state, every Ol has the mark of the Shadow Lord at its core, and whatever shape it takes, the mark will be somewhere on its body, in some form.

"The twins — the Ols we killed — each had a mark on the left cheekbone," said Lief. "Was that — ?"

Dain nodded. "But do not expect that it will always be so easy," he warned. "Grade Two Ols are far more expert. They never have the mark in plain view."

"You are saying, then," Barda put in, frowning, "that recognizing a Grade Two Ol is just a matter of luck?"

Dain smiled slightly. "There is a way of testing them," he said. "They cannot hold one shape for longer than three full days. If you observe a Grade Two Ol, and never let it out of your sight, there will come a moment when it loses control and its shape begins to change and waver. We call this moment the Tremor. It does not last long. In seconds the Ol has regained control. But by that time, you know it for what it is."

He was growing weary, hugging his chest with his good arm as though his pain was troubling him. "There are some in Deltora who do not have to wait for the Tremor," he said. "They have developed an instinct — a feeling for Ols. Or so Doom says. When he senses an Ol he strikes at once. I have never known him to be wrong."

"We can hardly follow his example," Barda muttered. "To kill just on suspicion is a risky business."

Dain nodded, and this time his smile was broader and more real. "I agree. For such as us, suspicion should be a signal to run, not strike."

"Run?" Jasmine demanded fiercely.

He flushed at the disdain in her voice, and the smile faded. "The idea displeases you, Jasmine. You and Doom are of one mind. But it is surely better to run than to kill an innocent person."

"Or," Barda put in, "if your suspicions are correct, to be spied upon by the Ol at its leisure, or killed when you least expect it. Once those icy fingers are around your throat, you are helpless. You can take my word for it, Jasmine." He touched his own bruised throat tenderly.

Jasmine lifted her chin stubbornly and turned again to Dain. "You have spoken of Grade One Ols, and Grade Twos. Are there other grades as well?"

Dain hesitated. "Doom says that there is another," he said reluctantly at last. "He says there are Grade Three Ols. He says they are few, but in them the Shadow Lord has perfected his evil art. They can change their shape to whatever they wish — living or nonliving. They are so perfect, so completely controlled, that no one could tell them for what they are. Even Doom could not."

"Then how does he know they exist at all?" Jasmine demanded.

Lief watched, fascinated, as Dain's eyelids drooped, and he bit his lip. What was troubling him?

Jasmine saw the hesitation, too, and pounced. "Well?" she insisted.

Dain swallowed. "Doom says — he says he learned of them — in the Shadowlands," he muttered.

Lief's stomach turned over. Suddenly it was as though parts of a puzzle were falling into place. Suddenly he was seeing a tombstone by an overgrown stream. Suddenly he was back in a cave on Dread Mountain, looking at some words scrawled in blood.

"When Doom says he has been in the Shadowlands, you do not believe him, Dain?" he asked.

Dain looked up, his eyes filled with confusion. "How can I?" he burst out. "No one escapes from the Shadowlands. Yet Doom never lies. Never!"

"He lies about his name!" Jasmine snapped.

"What do you mean?" Dain was very pale. He looked exhausted. His delicate face was beaded with sweat and deeply shadowed. He swayed.

Lief caught him before he fell. Barda found the Quality Brand jar and pushed a spoonful of honey between the closed lips. Soon a little color returned to the boy's face. Lief lowered him gently to the ground and covered him with a blanket.

"Do not worry, Dain," he said softly. "Whatever Doom's real name may be, he has not lied to you. He *has* been in the Shadowlands. And, somehow, he escaped. You may not believe it. But I do."

He saw Dain's eyelids flutter. The boy's mouth opened as though he was trying to speak. "We will talk of this again with Doom himself," Lief whispered. "For now, just rest. Tomorrow, you will need all your strength."

✳

Two long, hard days followed — days in which Lief's respect for Dain grew. The fall he had taken had not only sprained his arm, but had also cracked several ribs. By the second day they were climbing rocky hills. Every step Dain took must have caused him pain, yet he did not complain. Only his eyes revealed what he was suffering.

By now, the river was out of sight. Dread Mountain rose black and forbidding in the distance. Twice, looking back, Lief saw the huge, ungainly shape of an Ak-Baba circling it, searching for signs of travellers below.

In many ways, this was a welcome sign. It meant that the Shadow Lord, for all his power, did not realize that the companions had already taken the Mountain's gem. But the presence of an Ak-Baba, even at a distance, made the need for travelling under cover even more important. As the country became rougher, with straggling bushes and great boulders taking the place of lush trees, they were forced to crouch, shuffling along in single file.

For many hours Dain had not spoken. He seemed to need all his energy just to keep walking. How would he have fared alone? Lief thought, watching the boy's bowed back ahead of him, and hearing his shallow, painful breaths as he stumbled along.

"I think Dain needs rest," Lief called in a low voice.

Barda and Jasmine stopped at once, but Dain turned a little, shaking his head.

"We must get to safety. Then we can rest. It is not

far now," the boy gasped, holding his side with his uninjured arm. "Just up above . . . the cleft in the rock. Then — three bushes in a line, and — a cave entrance, sealed with a stone. There is a password . . . "

His voice trailed off. Then, without any warning, he fell heavily to the ground.

The three companions bent over him, calling his name, but he did not wake. Even the last of the honey did not revive him.

The sun dipped below the horizon, and the light dimmed.

"We must get him to shelter," Lief said. "Another night in the cold . . . "

"He said the stronghold was near," Barda muttered. "I will carry him the rest of the way." Gently he picked up the unconscious boy. Then they began clambering upward once more.

Soon they came to a deep crack in a rock — a crack like a narrow passageway. They scrambled through it and there, as Dain had said, were three bushes in a line, pointing to a boulder lying against a sheet of rock. The boulder looked quite natural, as though it had simply fallen where it lay, but they realized it must mask the entrance to the stronghold.

"It is well disguised," said Barda. "If we had not known where to look, we would have passed it by." He moved closer to the great rock and peered at it, looking for a means of moving it aside.

"It is strange that they have left no lookout," Jasmine murmured, looking around with her hand on her dagger. "They were surely expecting Dain's return. How was he supposed to get in?"

Lief looked around also, and noticed a strip of paper lying under the last of the bushes. It must have been blown there and become caught on a twig, he thought. He pulled it free and looked at it.

> WHEN ENEMIES AT PASS, ORDERS NORMAL

"Someone has been careless," he said grimly, showing the note to the others.

"They are expecting trouble, it seems," said Barda.

"It could be *us* they are expecting," Jasmine hissed. "We have only Dain's word for it that this is the Resistance stronghold. It could be a trap."

"We shall see." Lief snatched up a stout stick and moved to the boulder. He tapped it sharply, at the same time calling out: "Hello! We are friends, and ask entry."

There was silence behind the rock, but he had the strong feeling that someone was there. He tapped again.

"Doom, hear me! We are the travellers you saved from the Grey Guards near Rithmere. We have Dain with us. He is injured and needs shelter!"

"What is today's password?" called a deep, muffled voice. Startled, Lief stepped back. It was as though the rock itself had spoken. But soon he realized that the sound had come through a tiny crevice to the right of the boulder. Like the gnomes of Dread Mountain, the Resistance had peepholes in their walls.

"I wish to speak to Doom!" Lief shouted.

"Doom is not here," boomed the voice. "What is the password? Answer, or die."

4 - The Stronghold

Barda leaned closer to the stone. "Are you mad?" he shouted. "We are not enemies! We are known to Doom. And if you could see us you would know that we have your friend here."

"You *can* be seen, believe me," answered the voice behind the rock. "There are a dozen weapons aimed at you this moment. Do not move."

Startled, the companions looked around them. They could see no one. Jasmine took a step back. A ball of flame slammed into the ground beside her, showering her with sparks. She beat out the sparks frantically.

"I told you not to move!" called the voice. "Do so again at your peril."

"Call Neridah and Glock!" Jasmine called, her voice high with shock. "They are with you, I know.

Doom saved them from the Grey Guards, as he saved us. They will recognize our faces."

There was the sound of hollow laughter. "So they may. But in these parts we know better than to judge by appearances. That is why there is a password. Do you know it or not?"

"Of course!" Lief shouted.

"Lief!" hissed Jasmine.

"If I had said no, they would have killed us!" Lief hissed back. "They would have thought we were Ols!"

"They will kill us anyway, once they realize you are lying!" Jasmine's fists were clenched with frustration and anger. "This is madness!"

Lief shook his head desperately. "Dain mentioned a password. But he could not have known the password for today, for he has been long away. He must have planned to find it out once he got here. And if he could do that, so can we! There must be a code, a sign . . ."

"Where?" Jasmine demanded.

"Perhaps they all carry a list, with one word marked for every day," Barda said.

"That, surely, would be too dangerous," muttered Lief. "Still . . ." He threw Dain's pack to the ground and rapidly began searching through it. But as he expected he found nothing printed — only travellers' supplies, a few spare clothes, and the empty jar of Quality Brand honey.

Quality Brand.

He snatched up the jar and stared at it. Suddenly an idea had come to him. He scrabbled in his pocket for the note he had found under the bush.

"I grow tired of this game. You have the count of ten to reply!" called the voice from behind the rock. "One, two . . ."

"Wait!" Lief cried. His fingers closed on the note. He pulled it out and quickly read it again, hoping against hope that he was right. The printed words danced in front of his eyes.

WHEN ENEMIES AT PASS, ORDERS NORMAL.

Yes! What he saw here could surely not be just chance. He was right. Surely he was right. He took a deep breath and let the paper fall.

"The password is — 'weapon,' " he shouted.

"Lief, how do you know that?" hissed Barda. "What — "

He broke off as, slowly, the boulder that masked the stronghold's entrance began to roll aside, and light poured through the gap from the cavern within.

In the light stood a wiry little man wearing a strange assortment of garments in every color of the rainbow. Below his striped woollen cap, grey hair twisted with feathers hung to his waist.

Lief felt Barda give a start, but there was no time to ask him what was the matter, for the little man was grinning, showing two or three crooked teeth and a broad expanse of pink gums.

"You took your time!" he boomed, in the deep, powerful voice that did not suit his appearance at all. "Does it amuse you to dance with death? I was within a hair of giving the order to fire."

He peered shortsightedly at the limp figure in Barda's arms. "So the little boy has had an adventure and come to grief!" he said. "Well, well. Who would have thought it? And him always so careful of himself!"

As the companions hesitated, he beckoned impatiently. "Well, don't just stand there!" he exclaimed. "You are letting in the cold." He turned his head. "Thalgus! Petronne!" he bellowed. "All is well. Put down your weapons and come down. You must see to Dain. He has been carried home like a babe in arms, the poor poppet."

Lief and Jasmine slipped through the entrance. Barda followed more slowly. As he stepped into the light, the little man gazed up at his face and burst into noisy laughter. "Barda!" he roared. "Barda the Bear! Who would have believed it? After all these years! By my stars, I thought you were dead! Do you know me?"

"Of course I know you, Jinks," said Barda, smiling rather stiffly. "But this is the last place I would have expected to find you."

He paused as a roughly dressed man and an equally ragged woman — Thalgus and Petronne, presumably — jumped down to the ground from somewhere high above the doorway. He allowed them to take Dain's slight weight from his arms. Then he turned to Jasmine and Lief. "Jinks was one of the acrobats at the palace in Del," he explained, his voice revealing nothing. "He knew me well, when I was a palace guard."

"A palace guard? Why, the strongest and bravest of all, so it was said!" Jinks chattered, following Petronne and Thalgus as they carried Dain towards a larger cavern from which came the hum of many voices. "But Barda, I heard that all the guards were killed the day the Shadow Lord came. How did you escape the slaughter?"

"By chance I had left the palace before it began," Barda murmured. "And you?"

The little man wrinkled his nose. "The invaders cared nothing for the clowns and acrobats!" he jeered. "We were no more important than pet dogs to them. They let us scatter as we would. We tumbled over the wall while they shed the blood of fine lords and ladies, destroyed the palace guards, and took the place apart searching for our courageous king and queen, who were hiding somewhere trembling in their golden boots."

He grinned again, and this time the smile had a touch of teasing malice. "So! You managed to run away just in time to save yourself, Barda the Bear!" he crowed. "Cleverly done! Your fellows were all killed defending the palace, but not you! You must be very proud of yourself."

Lief glanced quickly at Barda and saw that his face had tightened with pain.

"Barda did not know what was going to happen that day!" he exclaimed angrily. "He left the palace the night before because his mother had been killed, and he feared he would be next!"

"Never mind, Lief," Barda muttered. He turned to Jinks, and Lief could tell that he was forcing himself to speak politely. "You would be doing me a great favor if you would not speak of my past to anyone else, Jinks. I prefer it to be secret."

The little man opened his eyes wide. "Why, of course, Barda!" he said smoothly. "I quite understand your position — even if your young friend does not. These are hard times, and we cannot all be heroes. Why, I myself am the world's greatest coward!" They reached the entrance to the larger cavern and he stood back, gesturing gracefully for them to enter. "Mind you, *I* do not pretend to be anything else," he added, as Barda passed him.

The cavern was large, lit by flickering torches and filled with groups of men, women, and children of many different ages. Food was already cooking on several fires, and straw mattresses lined the walls.

"Why do you let him call you a coward?" Jasmine whispered to Barda angrily, ignoring the faces turned to stare at the newcomers. "For that is what he is doing!"

"I am well aware of what he is doing," said

Barda grimly, staring straight ahead. "I know Jinks of old. He was a fine acrobat, but a more gossiping, jealous, spiteful, troublemaking piece of mischief was never born. Meeting him here is ill fortune indeed. Whatever he promises, by morning every person here will know everything about me."

"Dain already knows your name," Lief pointed out.

"The name is not so important," Barda growled. "The other details — "

He broke off as Jinks came bustling up to them, clapping his hands to gain the attention of everyone in the cavern.

"Here are some friends who have come to join us!" the little man cried. "They brought poor young Dain home. It seems he decided to go adventuring, and bit off more than he could chew."

He sniggered, glancing at the pale figure of Dain, who had been put down on a mattress of straw in a corner and was at last beginning to stir. Several other people laughed in reply, and Lief felt a hot flush of irritation. He opened his mouth to speak, but Jasmine was before him.

"Dain saved us from two Ols," she said loudly. "His bravery was very great."

"Is that so?" called a voice from the crowd. "Who are you to talk of bravery, Birdie of Bushtown?"

And out of the crowd pushed the swaggering, lumbering figure of Glock.

5 ~ Friend or Foe?

Glock stood sneering and glowering at Jasmine by turns, his powerful arms hanging loosely by his sides, his small eyes glinting. Every line of his powerful body showed that he was looking for a fight.

"Hello, Glock," said Jasmine calmly. "The last time I saw you, you were being carried out of the Rithmere arena, fast asleep. What a pity you could not stay awake for the final."

Several people laughed. Plainly they had heard the story. Glock's heavy face darkened and seemed to swell. He growled dangerously and his fingers twitched.

Out of the corner of his eye Lief saw Jinks watching, his face alive with mischievous interest. So Jinks was the sort who loved to stir up trouble, then stand back and watch the results. A dangerous man — as dangerous as Glock, in his way.

Just then there was the sound of banging from outside the cavern. Three slow taps, followed by three quick ones. Fleetingly, Jinks looked disappointed. Then he turned and scurried out, with Petronne and Thalgus close behind him.

"What is the password?" they heard him call.

"Weapon!" came the reply. The voice was muffled, but Lief thought he recognized it. Doom had returned.

Glock took no notice whatever. He was still intent on Jasmine.

"I should have been Champion, you little piece of slime!" he snarled. "If we had fought, your dancing, jumping tricks would not have deceived me. I would have crushed you to pulp with one hand tied behind my back!"

Jasmine stared at him in disgust. "Fortunately, your greed ensured that you did not have the chance to try," she said.

Glock roared, and grabbed at her. She sprang aside, smiling disdainfully as he stumbled, his great paws clawing at empty air.

"That is enough!"

Doom was standing, scowling, in the entrance. His face was seamed with lines of tiredness, his long, tangled black hair and beard were streaked with dust, and the jagged scar showed pale on his deeply tanned skin.

"There is to be no fighting in this place!" he thundered. "Glock, you have been warned before. One more outburst and you will be turned out of the stronghold. Then you will no longer be under our protection when the Grey Guards come for you."

Glock turned and lumbered off, grumbling and casting evil looks over his shoulder. No one made a sound, but Lief saw a tall woman put her hand over her mouth to hide a smile. The woman was Neridah. She saw Lief watching, and her smile grew broader and more teasing. He looked away, his face growing hot as he remembered the shame she had caused him in the Rithmere arena.

Doom's angry eyes were now fixed on Jasmine. "And you," he added coldly, "will guard your sharp tongue, if you know what is good for you."

In the silence that followed he turned abruptly and went to the mattress where Dain was resting. By now, the boy had managed to sit up.

"So," Doom said. "You have returned at last, Dain. You were expected days ago. Where have you been?"

Dain flushed deep red. "I saw a pair of Ols, Doom," he mumbled. "Grade One only. I followed them — "

"Alone!" Doom snapped. "You followed them

alone. You went out of your way, disobeying orders, failing to arrive here when expected."

Dain hung his head. But Doom had not finished. "And I have been told" — he glanced at Jinks, who tried and failed to look innocent — "I have been told that you chose to endanger all our lives by telling these untested strangers the secret of the password."

There was an angry murmuring in the cavern.

Finally Dain found his tongue. "Indeed — indeed I did not tell them, Doom," he said.

"Then how did they gain entry?" Doom's voice was icy. "You, I gather, did not even see today's note. Yet they were able to give the word."

"It was not difficult to work out," Lief said, stepping forward hastily. "The note said, 'WHEN ENE-MIES AT PASS, ORDERS NORMAL.' The first letters of those words spell the password — 'WEAPON.' "

As Doom glared at him, he shrugged and threw caution to the winds. He was not going to be bullied like Dain. "I had a clue to the code, of course," he said loudly. "I had already seen the label on Dain's jar of honey. 'Quality Brand.' There, too, initials are used to disguise the truth. Why are you afraid for it to be known that you use Queen Bee honey?"

Another loud murmur arose from the crowd. Doom barked an order and immediately Lief, Barda, and Jasmine were seized from behind by several pairs of strong hands. They struggled, but it was no use.

"What are you doing?" Lief spluttered. "I meant no harm by my question! I was simply interested."

"Then you would have done better to hold your tongue," said Doom, his eyes hard as stones. "You have stumbled on a secret we are sworn to protect. It is forbidden to trade with the Resistance. And Queen Bee honey is even more rare and valuable than Queen Bee cider. It has amazing healing powers. The lady risks much by supplying it to us. She risks not only her own life, but the lives of her sons."

Now it was Lief's turn to stare. The idea of the wild old woman they had met after their escape from the Plain of the Rats being a mother seemed very strange.

"It is nothing to us if Queen Bee supplies you with honey," growled Barda. "Who would we tell?"

"Your Master, perhaps," called Jinks, his small eyes gleaming with excitement. "Is that why you were allowed to escape from the palace, Brave Guard Barda? Had you sold yourself to the Shadow Lord even then?"

Barda lunged forward in fury, but the hands that held him jerked him back.

"Be silent, Jinks!" roared Doom. He gazed at Barda thoughtfully for a moment.

"So," he murmured. "You were a palace guard. Your real name is Barda. And where were you hiding for all those years, Barda — before you began travelling the countryside with your young companions?"

"That is my affair," said Barda, meeting his eyes squarely. "I choose to keep it to myself. As, I think, you choose to keep to yourself your own whereabouts in those early years, Doom."

"Your whereabouts — *and* your real name," Jasmine muttered.

Doom glanced at her quickly. His mouth tightened. He turned once again to Barda.

"Were you in Tora?" he asked bluntly.

At this, Dain, who had been slumped on the mattress with his head bowed, looked up eagerly.

But Barda looked blank. "Tora?" he repeated. "What is this fascination with Tora, among you? No, I have never been to Tora in my life."

Doom abruptly turned away. "Take them to the testing room," he snapped. "I will speak to them again when the three days have passed."

"Let us go!" Jasmine shouted, as they were dragged to the cavern door. "There is no reason to imprison us! You know that we are not Ols! You know it!"

Doom lifted his chin. "We shall see," he said.

※

Locked in the small, brightly lit cave that Doom called "the testing room," the three companions spent three weary days. A barred window was set into the heavy wooden door, and at all times a face stared through it, watching their every move.

Their possessions were with them. Even their

weapons had not been taken from them. Trays of food were pushed under the door, and they had plenty of water. But there was no privacy, no darkness, no peace.

By the third day even Barda was desperate. Jasmine lay curled on a bunk, her hands over her face. Kree sat in a corner of the cell, his wings drooping. Lief paced in an agony of impatience, feeling time tick away.

He cursed the day they had met Dain — then remembered that if it had not been for Dain, he, Barda, and Jasmine would all be dead. He cursed Doom's suspicion — then remembered his own shock when sweet little Marie had changed to a specter bent on killing.

But had Dain not said that Doom could sense an Ol? If so, then Doom knew full well that Lief, Barda, and Jasmine were what they seemed. Why then, was he keeping them here?

He wants to keep us by him. The three-day test is an excuse — something the others in the cavern will accept and understand. He wants to know what we are up to. He hopes that after this we will tell him.

The idea shone clearly in Lief's mind. He knew it was the truth.

Well, you are wrong, Doom, or whatever your name may be, he thought grimly. We will never tell you of our cause. And that is because we still do not know whether you are friend, or foe.

They had lost track of time. They did not know whether it was day or night. But it was in fact exactly seventy-two hours and five minutes after they first entered the cavern that they heard a hiss from the window in the door.

Peering through the bars was Dain, no longer bent with pain, but upright, and with his arm free of its sling. His face was set and determined, though Lief saw that the fingers resting on the window were trembling.

"The three days have passed," he whispered, as the three companions gathered by the door. "You no longer need to be watched. But Doom still delays setting you free. I do not know why, and I feel it is not right. I will lead you out of here. But only if you promise me that you will take me with you. To Tora."

6 - A Change of Plans

Dain may have been afraid — may, indeed, have been guilty and ashamed — to free Lief, Barda, and Jasmine from the cell and lead them in silence down the dark passage beyond. He may have trembled as they moved into another tunnel and on to a small door that opened to the outside world. But still, he did it. And when they stood at last in the open air, under stars that sparkled like jewels scattered over the black velvet tent of the sky, he heaved a sigh of relief.

"We are safe, now," he whispered. "They are all eating and drinking. No one will visit the testing room again until it is the hour for sleep. By then, we can be long gone."

They wasted no time with words, but together began scrambling away over the rocks, slipping and sliding on loose stones, catching hold of rough bushes to stop themselves from falling.

Only when they were well away from the stronghold, when they were on flat ground again, did they stop to rest, and talk.

"Tora is many days' journey downriver from here," whispered Dain. "We will have to take great care as we go. Bandits and pirates haunt the River Tor, and Ols patrol the area in great numbers."

"Why?" whispered Lief in reply. "What is so special about Tora, Dain? And why do you want to go there?"

Dain stared at him. Several expressions seemed to chase themselves across his face: surprise, bewilderment, disbelief, and finally, anger. Slowly he clambered to his feet.

"You know very well why," he hissed, looking Lief up and down. "Can it be that still you do not trust me?" He shook his head violently from side to side. "I have betrayed my people for you. I have betrayed Doom, who has been like a father to me! Is that not enough to prove — ?"

"Be still, boy," muttered Barda. "It is not a matter of trust. We know very little of Tora."

"I know nothing of it," Jasmine muttered. "I had never heard of it until you said its name when we first met."

"But I thought — " Dain took a deep, shuddering breath and pressed his hands together till the knuckles showed white. "You tricked me. You told me you were going — "

"We told you nothing," Barda said firmly. "*You* suggested that Tora was our goal. We simply did not correct your mistake."

Dain groaned and buried his face in his hands. It was dark, and he moved swiftly, but Lief thought he saw the dark eyes shining with tears. He felt a pang of guilt, and put a careful hand on Dain's shoulder.

"We are going all the way to the coast, following the river. If Tora is on the river, or near it, we can escort you there, if that is what you wish."

Still with his face in his hands, Dain slowly shook his head from side to side. "When first I heard of you — a man, a boy, and a wild girl with a black bird, in whose presence the Shadow Lord's evil was undone — I began to think you were the answer," he said, his voice thick and muffled. "And as the months went by, and Doom brought news that you were moving west, I became sure of it."

He stifled a sob. "Then I met you. I thought it was fate. But it has all been a mistake. Another mistake. Oh, I can do nothing right! What am I to do?"

"I think you had better tell us what is troubling you," said Jasmine flatly. "No purpose is served by wailing and grieving."

Dain looked up. Her calm seemed to have brought him to himself as no amount of kind sympathy could ever do. He rubbed the back of his hand over his eyes, wiping away the tears.

"For reasons I cannot tell you, I must get to Tora. But Doom forbids it. At first — when first he found me — left for dead after bandits burned my family's farm — he said I must regain my strength. Then he said I needed more training to travel in safety, though already I could use a bow. Later he said he needed my help for just a little while, and I could not refuse him. And at last, as I grew impatient, he said that Tora had grown too dangerous for me or any of our group, until we were much stronger."

He paused, shaking his head as if to clear it. "He says that to visit it now would mean certain capture, and this would be a danger to the whole Resistance. He says Tora is crawling with Grey Guards and thick with spies, because . . ."

His voice trailed off, and he swallowed.

"Because Tora has always been so loyal to the royal family," said Barda suddenly. "Of course!"

His eyes were alert and excited. In the back of Lief's mind, memory stirred. The memory was of his father, beating red-hot iron in the forge, talking of Tora, the great city of the west. He had said that it was a place of beauty, culture, and powerful magic, far away from bustling Del and its palace, but fiercely loyal to the crown. Lief remembered his father describing a painting he had seen in the palace library, long ago.

It was a picture of a great crowd of people. All

were tall and slender, with long, smooth faces, slanting eyebrows, dark eyes, and shining black hair. They wore robes of many colors, with deep sleeves that touched the ground. Their hands were pressed over their hearts.

They were all facing a huge rock from the top of which green flames sprang high into the sky. Beside the rock, his head bowed humbly, stood a big man in rough working clothes, wearing the Belt of Deltora. A beautiful, black-haired woman stood beside him, her hand on his arm.

"Adin loved a Toran woman, and she loved him," Lief said slowly. "When he was proclaimed king, she went with him to Del, to rule by his side. On the day they left, the Torans swore allegiance to Adin, and all who came after him. Other tribes had done the same, but the Torans, who were the greatest among them, carved their oath upon the flaming rock that stood at their city's heart, and set a spell upon it that could never be broken."

He met Barda and Jasmine's eyes, and the same thought flashed between them. What more perfect place than Tora to hide the heir to the throne?

"It is a long way from Del to Tora," said Barda aloud, choosing his words carefully so as not to reveal their meaning to Dain. "A perilous journey. But once there . . ."

Yes, Lief's eyes answered silently. Once there, King Endon could have been quite sure of help. The

Torans would have done anything, risked anything, to keep him, Queen Sharn, and their baby safe. And they had magic enough to do it — whatever the Shadow Lord threatened, whatever destruction he caused.

"You *do* know something of Tora, then!" Dain was exclaiming, his face brightening.

"Not as it is now," Lief said slowly. "I know only the ancient stories. No news has reached Del from the west since before I was born."

"And perhaps long before that," Barda put in. He met Dain's anxious eyes. "I think, perhaps, that it is not only the dangers of Tora that cause Doom to forbid it to his people. It is also Tora's loyalty to the crown. Doom wants no part of that. He despises the memory of the royal family. Is that not so?"

Dain's shoulders slumped. "It is so," he admitted. "And Doom wants no part of Tora's magic, either. He says we depended on magic to save us in the past, and that it failed us. He says that we must learn to stand on our own feet, and fight the Shadow Lord with cunning, strength, and weapons. But I — "

"You know that is not enough," Lief broke in. "And it is you who are right, Dain. The Enemy's power was gained by sorcery. Ordinary strength, however determined, may undo some of his evil work, but can never defeat him for good."

Jasmine had been listening, looking from one speaker to another. Now she spoke.

"Ordinary strength may not defeat the Shadow

Lord. But ordinary sense tells us how we must proceed from here. Plainly, we are about to travel into territory the Enemy is watching closely. There will be many eyes watching for the group they have been told about — a man, a boy — and a wild girl with a black bird."

She said the last words with a bitter smile.

Lief tried to interrupt, but she held up her hand to stop him. "We must separate, if we are not to be noticed," she said. "And since Kree and I are the ones who make our group obvious, we are the ones who must take another path."

She pulled on her pack. Kree flew to perch on her arm. Filli chattered fearfully.

"Jasmine, no!" Lief exclaimed.

"Do not leave us!" cried Dain at the same moment.

Jasmine turned to Barda. "I am right, am I not?" she demanded. "Tell them!"

The big man hesitated, but his grieved face showed that he knew her reasoning was sound.

She nodded briskly. "Then that is settled. All being well, we will meet on the coast, at the river's end."

With that, she lifted a hand in farewell and moved quickly off into the darkness. With a cry Lief started after her. But she did not answer his call, and he could not catch her. In moments she was just a flickering shadow among the trees. Then she was gone.

7 ~ Where Waters Meet

Barda, Lief, and Dain were following the river, creeping through the trees that ran along its banks.

Many days had passed since Jasmine had left them, and though Lief watched constantly for signs of her, so far he had seen nothing. It was strange and dull to be travelling without her, without Filli's soft chatter in the background and Kree squawking above their heads. Dain, though always dependable in time of trouble, could not take her place.

Lief was alarmed, too, to realize how much he and Barda had grown to depend on Jasmine's sharp eyes and hearing to warn them of approaching danger. For there was danger in plenty. Twice the companions had been forced to fight for their lives when bandits took them by surprise, leaping down on them from the trees. Four times they had hidden just in time as pirate boats sailed by — large, battered wooden craft patched with all manner of odd bits and pieces, some of them with sails made of scraps of cloth roughly sewn together.

The ruffians who hoisted the sails, lay sleeping on the rough boards, or plied the long oars, were as ill-assorted as the materials that made their craft. They were of every size, color, and shape, but all had a savage, hungry look. Their clothes were ragged and filthy and their hair wild, but the knives, swords, and axes that hung from their belts gleamed sharp and bright in the sun.

A lone figure swayed at the top of every mast, strapped in place with ropes or supported on a sling of leather. From that high perch, hard eyes, shaded with a hand, hat, or branch of leaves, scanned the riverbanks and the water ahead.

Looking for prey. Looking for travellers to kill and rob. Looking for unprotected villages, for other boats to plunder.

Here, far from the mountains and the streams that fed it, the river had grown slow, narrow, and winding. It was dark and oily, flecked with evil-looking foam. The smell of death and decay hung over it like mist. Rotting, broken timbers, rags of clothing, and other rubbish bobbed in its current.

There were more sinister floating things, too. Now and again dead bodies drifted just below the surface, the water around them swirling and bubbling horribly as writhing river creatures feasted unseen.

And Ols? Who knew which bandits, which creatures, were Ols?

One evening, when Lief, Barda, and Dain had stopped for the night, two beautiful water birds, purest white, waded through the reeds to shore, bending their graceful necks as if asking to be fed. But they ignored the scraps Lief threw to them. They simply stared. And only when they raised their wings to fly away did Lief see the black spot each bore on its side, and realize what they were.

Prowling Ols. But a man and two boys were of no interest to them. They were moving on, to seek the man, the boy, the girl, and the black bird they had been sent to find and destroy.

Lief lay back, his stomach churning, staring at the brightness of the moon. In three days it would be full, and even now it was large and gleaming, lighting the darkness. Every bush seemed bright. Every tree was open to view. There were no hiding places.

Jasmine had been right. It was her presence, and Kree's, that made their group stand out. But if the Ols found her alone, with Kree by her side, would they not strike? She was the one in true danger now.

Lief prayed she would be safe. He vowed to himself that if they all survived this test, their party would never again be separated. Prudence was all very fine. But other things were more important.

✳

The next morning they reached a bridge that spanned another river flowing into the Tor. The bridge was arched high so that boats could sail under it, and, though in bad repair, it felt safe enough to cross. On the other side was a tiny village, nestling in the corner made by the two rivers. It seemed deserted.

"This is Broad River, I think," said Dain, looking down at the slow-moving water as they began to cross the bridge. "You would have seen part of it on your way to Rithmere."

"Oh, yes," Barda answered with a grim smile. "And felt it, too — more than we would like. So this is where it ends."

They reached the end of the bridge and began to move towards the village, which they could now see had suffered some terrible disaster. Many houses had been burned. Windows were shattered. Rubble and broken glass littered the narrow streets.

"Pirates," Dain muttered.

There was a post sticking up from the ground ahead, and when they reached it they saw that it had once supported a sign. Now the sign lay on the ground, its edges broken, its brave lettering muddied.

Where Waters Meet

Welcome, Travellers!

"I have heard Doom speak of this place," said Dain dully. "He said the people were brave and full of good heart. He wanted them to join us, so they would be safe. But they refused to abandon their village to the pirates. They said they would defend it with their last breath."

"It seems they did so." Barda's voice was harsh with anger.

As Lief began to turn away, he saw that some scraps of thick yellow knitting wool had fallen on the bare ground along the board's top edge. He crouched to pick them up — then snatched his hand back as he saw that they were arranged in a pattern.

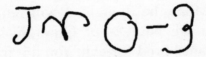

"Barda! Jasmine has been here!" he exclaimed excitedly." And perhaps she is here still. This is a message for us — a message no other person would notice. See? She has made the first letter of her name. And a picture of a bird for Kree. The other signs must tell us where she is sheltering."

Barda considered the shapes on the ground. "The circle could be part of a building. But what is the 3?"

"A number on a door, perhaps!" Lief stood up and looked around, filled with new energy.

With Dain trailing behind them, they began to

explore the village. It was a depressing task, and Lief's excitement quickly died. Plainly, Where Waters Meet had once been a busy, thriving little town. Now, everywhere were the signs of violence and bloodshed. The tavern, the meeting hall, every house, every shop, had been ransacked. Everything of any value had been taken.

Some of the invaders had scrawled their names triumphantly on the walls of living rooms, bedrooms, and halls. "Nak" was one name that occurred again and again, twice in what looked like blood. But there were other names, too. "Finn" was one, "Milne" another.

Lief stared at the scrawlings with hatred. Nak, Finn, and Milne, he thought, I will remember your names. You are not Ols or Grey Guards, Shadow Lord's servants, bred for evil. You are free to choose how you act. And you have chosen to prey upon your own people. You have chosen to steal, destroy, and murder. I hope that, one day, I meet you. Then I will make you pay.

With heavy hearts they finished searching. There was a circular courtyard, and some window frames in the shape of circles, too. But there were no numbers at all, and there was no sign of Jasmine.

Lief stopped outside the last house, which had a new moon carved into the door. "Moons are circles, when they are full," he called to Barda. "Could Jasmine have meant — ?"

Then he broke off, for he had at last realized the true meaning of Jasmine's message. He shook his head, annoyed at his own slowness. "We have been wasting our time," he exclaimed. "Jasmine is long gone. The signs tell us not where she is in Where Waters Meet, but when she was here. The circle is the full moon. Then there is a minus sign, and the number 3. She was here yesterday — three days before full moon!"

"Of course!" Barda heaved a great sigh. "Then — "

Suddenly he looked alert, and put his finger to his lips, listening. Lief listened in his turn and heard the last thing he would have expected.

It was the jingling of many tiny bells, growing louder. And, even more astonishing, the merry, booming sound of someone singing.

Once there was an Ol-io,
Jolly-wolly Ol-io,
Once there was an Ol-io,
Fearsome as could be!

I said to that Ol-io,
Jolly-wolly Ol-io,
I said to that Ol-io,
You don't bother me!

8 ~ Steven

A shabby caravan pulled by a fat old horse was trundling towards the village along the Broad River path. At first, Lief thought there were two figures sitting on the driver's seat. But as the caravan drew closer he saw that he had been mistaken. There was only one — a huge golden-haired man with dark brown skin, singing his rather surprising song at the top of his voice.

Impulsively Lief moved forward. "Wait," Barda muttered. "Looks and words can be deceiving."

Lief nodded, and stayed where he was. But when he heard the man's song falter as the caravan drew up to the ruined town sign, and saw the sorrow on the broad face, he was not willing to wait any longer.

The man's mouth turned down as he saw the three emerge from the shadows. "Ah," he said. "This is a bad business." He climbed down from the caravan and looked around him, taking in the desolation. "But I am not surprised. Every year for many years we have come here on our rounds, and each time I have feared finding this very thing."

He shook his head. "I warned them. I said to them, 'Give it up, my friends. Move on! Life is precious!' But they were so brave. So foolish . . ."

He rubbed a huge hand over his eyes.

"You speak of your rounds," said Barda, who was still wary. "What rounds?"

The man looked up. "Why, I am a peddler, sir," he said politely. "I sell, I buy, and I trade. Steven B is my name." He gestured at the faded lettering on his cart.

To Lief's surprise, there was a movement behind him and Dain stepped forward.

"Hello, Steven," the boy said. "Do you not know me?"

The man's face relaxed into a grin. "Young Dain!" he said. "I saw you there, but I was not sure you wished to be recognized in this company."

"These are friends," said Dain. "They are helping me on my way to Tora, Steven. I am going there at last."

The grin faded. "These are bad tidings," Steven said. "Why do you not stay where you are safe? This part of the country is not kind to travellers."

"Yet you travel every day," Lief pointed out.

Steven shrugged his massive shoulders. "I?" he said, as if that was another matter altogether. "Ah, yes. But I have protection."

Lief stared. The man was unarmed, and seemed quite alone except for the old horse. He was big, certainly, but his pleasant, open face did not seem the face of a fighter. Quite the opposite.

"Steven's brother, Nevets, always travels with him," said Dain quickly, and, Lief thought, warningly.

Steven put his head on one side. "Would you like to meet Nevets?" he enquired.

"Oh, no. We would not dream of disturbing him," Dain exclaimed, before Lief and Barda could say anything. "But, before you go, my friends and I would like to buy some goods for our journey, Steven."

The man beamed. "A pleasure to serve you," he

said. He strode to the back of the caravan and threw open the doors. The space was fitted out as a tiny shop, crammed with clothes and household needs.

The brother is not hiding in here, in any case, thought Lief. And what are we to buy? For, plainly, we are expected to buy something.

He watched as Dain bought a small cooking pot he did not need. Then Steven turned to him. "And what is your fancy, sir?" Steven asked.

Lief held out a coin and gestured to a basket containing many small packets of what looked like toffee. Steven raised his eyebrows, but took the coin and tossed him two packets.

Then it was Barda's turn, and to Lief's surprise Barda pointed to a wide cloth belt embroidered with a pattern of dull gold and brown leaves. "If that is within my means, I will take it," Barda said.

"A fine choice," said Steven, removing the belt from its hook. "And to you, a friend of Dain's, only three silver coins." He measured Barda's waist with his eyes. "You could find it a little snug, however," he added.

"It is not for me," said Barda, counting out the money. "It is a gift."

Steven nodded and passed over the belt. "Ah, well," he said. "Our journey has not been quite without profit, and that is one good thing. But this place makes me sad, and that will never do. We will stay no longer."

As he turned away to close the doors, he began mumbling to himself. A strange character, Lief thought. And a little mad, for this brother he speaks of seems to exist only in his imagination. Perhaps Nevets died, and this turned Steven's wits.

Steven finished bolting the doors, and walked to the front of the caravan. As he put his foot on the step to climb up to the driver's seat, he turned back to Dain. "Give up this idea of Tora, for now, Dain, and come with us," he said, stretching out a friendly hand. "There is room on the seat for you. Soon we will be meeting with some of your friends, to make a delivery. You could return to the stronghold with them."

Dain shook his head. "I thank you most sincerely for the offer, Steven," he said. "But I cannot accept."

Steven looked regretful, then shrugged and finished his climb. When he was safely on the driver's seat again, he bent and fumbled underneath it. There was a clinking sound, and at last he brought out a small jar. This he passed to Dain. "With my compliments," he said. "May it help you on your journey."

As Dain stammered his thanks, Lief looked curiously at the jar. With a small shock, he saw the familiar "Quality Brand Honey" label.

Steven saw him looking, and put a finger to the side of his nose. "Not a word," he said. He clicked to the horse. The caravan lurched forward, and slowly turned until it was facing the way it had come.

Barda, Lief, and Dain raised their hands in

farewell. Steven grinned and waved. Then he shook the jingling reins and the caravan creaked away.

"He sells Queen Bee honey?" Lief muttered. "But I thought it was in short supply."

"He sells only to the Resistance," said Dain, looking down at the jar. "And then he charges only a fraction of the honey's worth. Do you not understand? He is no ordinary peddler. He is the son of Queen Bee herself."

Lief drew a quick breath.

"But what was this talk of a brother?" Barda demanded. "He was alone!"

A cloud seemed to pass over Dain's face. "Steven is never alone," he said. "Nevets is always with him. But Nevets is not a man you would like to meet. I have seen him only once, and I never want to do so again."

As they stared, he turned to look after the caravan. "Nevets only appears when Steven, or someone close to him is threatened. Most of the time he stays within."

Barda shook his head impatiently. "There was no one within!" he snorted. "The caravan contained only goods for sale."

"Not within the caravan," murmured Dain. "Within Steven himself."

Lief felt the hairs rise on the back of his neck. He peered along the path. The caravan was almost hidden by a fine cloud of dust. But the jingling of the bells on the horse's reins floated back to him. And over the bells came the sound of singing.

> *Colly-wobble Ol-io,*
> *Jolly-wolly Ol-io,*
> *Colly-wobble Ol-io,*
> *You don't bother me!*

But this time, Lief could have sworn that instead of one voice, there were two.

9 - Onward

As soon as the caravan was out of sight, the companions turned their backs on the sad remains of Where Waters Meet and picked their way down to the bank of the River Tor. There they came upon a small wooden jetty that pushed out a little way over the water. On a pole was fixed a metal sign.

River Queen

"A passenger boat must work on this part of the Tor. It must come down Broad River, carrying travellers and goods to Tora," exclaimed Lief. "That is why the bridge is built so high. Dain, have you heard of this?"

Dain shook his head, eyeing the sign suspiciously.

"It would be very nice to ride instead of walking, for a change — and faster, too," Lief said. "Should we wait?"

Barda shook his head regretfully. "I think not. For all we know the boat comes by only once a week — or perhaps no longer runs at all. This sign is not new. And in any case, we have decided to keep away from public view."

Reluctantly Lief agreed, and they trudged on.

After the joining of the rivers, the Tor broadened, deepened, and grew less winding. It looked cleaner, too, and the smell of decay was less. But Lief knew that beneath the smooth surface dark shapes, and pale ones, too, were slowly drifting. They had not disappeared, only sunk out of sight.

As the river broadened, the country on their side also changed. Gradually the trees and bushes disappeared, the reeds thickened. By the time the companions stopped for the night, the earth beneath their feet had grown marshy.

After they had eaten, Dain settled at once to sleep. The bright moon rose. Lief remembered the packets he had bought from Steven, and pulled one out, intending to share the toffee with Barda. But as soon as he had unwrapped the hard, shiny brown stuff inside he realized that, whatever it was, it was not toffee. It smelled vile, and tasted worse.

Embarrassed to have made such a stupid mistake, Lief wrapped it up again and pushed it deep into his pocket. He glanced at Barda to see if he had noticed, but Barda was busy examining his own purchase, the embroidered belt. As Lief watched curiously, wondering who the gift was for, Barda looked up and beckoned. Carefully, so as not to wake Dain, Lief crept over to him.

"I bought this belt for a reason, Lief," Barda murmured. "The cloth is double, thick, and strong. I believe we should use it — as a covering for the Belt of Deltora."

Lief opened his mouth to protest. If the Belt was enclosed by cloth, he would not be able to touch and see the gems. He would lose the value of the topaz, that sharpened the mind; the ruby, that paled at danger — and the opal, that gave glimpses of the future.

He feared the power of the opal, but for days he had been trying to screw up his courage to touch it. His father's map showed that the Maze of the Beast was on Deltora's west coast, but its actual location was unclear. The opal might provide a clue.

"The river is thick with enemies. And Dain is with us, at least as far as Tora," Barda continued. "It will only be a matter of time before he, at least, sees the Belt, however careful you are."

Lief choked back his protest. Barda was right. He felt truly sorry for Dain, but the fact remained that neither he nor Barda could yet make up their minds to trust him completely. He nodded, and Barda at once set about splitting the seam of the embroidered belt.

Lief gritted his teeth. Time was short. He could delay no longer. He slipped his hands under his shirt and ran his fingers over the gems until he came to the opal.

Eerie, bluish light. Great dripping spears of stone hanging from the roof. Gleaming, ridged walls, running with milky liquid. And something huge, white, with thrashing tail, bloodred jaws gaping . . .

Gasping, Lief tore his hands free. He screwed his eyes tightly shut, trying to dismiss the horrible picture from his mind.

"Lief?"

Barda was holding out his hand impatiently. With trembling fingers Lief pulled off the Belt. Barda slipped it inside the embroidered band and began sewing up the split. When he had finished, there was nothing to show that any work had been done at all.

Lief buckled the cloth band around his waist, under his shirt. It felt rough and strange against his skin. Father kept the Belt safe inside a leather working belt for sixteen years, he thought. This is a sensible plan.

But still he felt uneasy. He returned to the camp-fire and lay down to sleep, wishing heartily, and not for the first time, that Dain had never crossed their path.

✳

The next morning the companions struggled on, but by midday they were staggering instead of walking, plunging knee-deep into foul-smelling mud with every step.

"This is impossible," panted Barda after another hour in which very little ground had been covered. "We will have to move away from the river — get to drier land."

But by now the reed beds extended as far as the eye could see. Heavy fog blotted out the horizon. They seemed surrounded by a wet, stinking desert of mud.

It was then that they heard a faint chugging, and the sound of music. They all turned to look upstream. Coming towards them, steam puffing from its funnel, its great paddle wheel churning the water behind it, was a red-painted boat.

Lief, Barda, and Dain did not hesitate. All of them began to shout, waving their arms.

The boat came nearer. Soon it was so close that they could see the name *River Queen* painted in bright white letters on its bow. And over the music they could hear the shouts of a bearded man in a captain's cap who leaned over the side, peering at them.

"Want a ride, mates?" he roared, as the boat slowed.

"Yes!" shouted Lief, Barda, and Dain.

"Do you have money?"

"Yes!"

The man grinned. "Never let it be said that the *River Queen* turned away a paying passenger. Let alone three. Ho, Chett!"

With that, a small rowing boat splashed into the water. A strange, hunched creature with long arms and a grinning, hairy face leaped into the boat and began rowing furiously to shore.

"What is that?" whispered Lief.

"A polypan," said Dain, wrinkling his nose and taking a step back. "And if this captain uses polypans as crew, he is up to no good."

"I believe I saw something like it in the markets at Rithmere," said Barda. "It was moving around the crowd with a cup, collecting money for a woman who was playing the violin."

Dain nodded. "And secretly collecting far more than that, no doubt," he muttered, as the little boat approached. "Polypans are expert thieves. It is said that they can take the shirt off your back without your knowledge."

The rowing boat ran aground on the mud and the polypan beckoned, grinning widely. Lief saw that it was chewing some sort of dark-colored gum. Its teeth were stained brown and as the companions waded through the reeds towards it, it spat a gob of brown liquid into the river.

Lief and Dain climbed into the boat. Barda pushed it off the mud and then climbed in after them.

The polypan spat again, and then began rowing back to the *River Queen*. Though it was now carrying three extra people, the little boat ploughed through the water at great speed. The polypan's long, hairy arms were very powerful, and it seemed to have boundless energy.

When they reached the side of the larger boat, they found that a rope ladder had been lowered over the side. They began to climb upward, one after the other, very aware of the polypan's little black eyes fixed on them. No doubt, thought Lief uncomfortably, it was noting every pocket in their jackets, every fastening on their packs.

He felt glad that the Belt of Deltora was safely hidden. His only regret was that now it could not tell him if the feeling of danger that flooded over him the moment he set foot on the boat's deck was real, or imagined.

10 ~ The *River Queen*

The other passengers stared curiously at the new-comers. One, a hugely fat man in a striped jersey, was clutching a large painted box with a handle. A music box, Lief guessed, remembering the music he had heard from the shore. "Ho-di-ho!" the fat man cried, in a strangely light, shrill voice for one so large. "Lockie the Stripe at your service, music-lovers!"

The woman beside him giggled. She was also quite plump, and was wearing a pink dress and mittens. Her round face was framed by huge bunches of pink curls that clustered over her forehead and cheeks. With one hand she waved girlishly at Lief, Barda, and Dain. With the other she nudged the arm of a tall, thin man with a patch over one eye who stood by her side. He nodded gravely.

Two other men looked up from a table where they

had been playing cards, but made no attempt to speak. They both had shaved heads, and had broad bands tied around their brows. Their fingers were covered in rings, and each had what looked like an animal tooth stuck through one ear. They did not look friendly.

The last passenger was a haughty-looking young woman in a fine purple cloak tied at the throat with golden cord. The hands that held her golden parasol were tightly gloved in black to match her shining high-heeled boots. A scarf of purple silk was bound closely around her head. Long golden earrings swung from her ears. Her face was powdered white, her lips were painted red, and her eyes were outlined heavily in black. After one bored glance at the newcomers she turned away and stared out at the water, twirling her parasol.

Lief looked around, trying to appear at ease. But his heart was sinking. Any one of these characters could be an Ol. They could all be Ols, come to that. He began to wonder if he, Barda, and Dain would have been better off remaining in the reed beds.

The captain strode up, grinning. He was a short, chunky man with a twisted nose and grey hair in a thick braid that hung down his back like a rope. His peaked cap was pulled so low on his forehead that his eyes were in deep shadow. "Welcome aboard! How far will you be going?" he asked.

"One of my sons and I have business on the coast," Barda said pleasantly.

"Is that so?" grinned the captain. "Fishy business, I've no doubt." He nudged Barda knowingly, then stuck out a filthy hand for payment. As Barda counted out the coins, Lief saw that the captain's little finger was missing, and the ring finger was just a stump.

"A little argument with a big worm, lad," said the captain, noticing that Lief was looking at his hand. "You'll want to keep your own little pinkies out of the water as we get on. The worms, they swim up from the sea. And the farther in they get, the hungrier they get." He grinned, and the woman in pink giggled nervously.

"My younger son wishes to stop off in Tora," Barda said, raising his voice slightly. "Can you oblige him?"

"Tora?" The captain snorted with laughter. "Why, no. I can't oblige the young fellow there, I fear. A visit to Tora is not possible for us."

Dain gave a start, but instantly controlled himself. Plainly, he had decided that he had no choice but to stay with the boat, at least for the present.

Barda looked at him, then shrugged agreement.

"All right. Only two more things," the captain went on. "One, I'm offering a ride, not a guard service. This is a cruel river, and your safety is your own concern. Two, if you're Ols, that's your business. I'll carry Ols as happily as I'll carry anyone, as long as they pay. But you'll keep your hands to yourselves while you're on this boat, or you'll find yourselves overboard feeding the worms. I've dealt with Ols before, and I can do it again. Understand?"

Lief, Barda, and Dain stared, then nodded. The captain grinned, turned on his heel, and left them.

"It's all right," hissed the woman in pink. "He said that to us, too. I suppose he has to be careful. But really!"

The captain had returned to the helm in the boat's cabin. He shouted some orders, the polypan leaped to do his bidding, a whistle sounded, and the boat began moving again.

Lockie the Stripe sat down with a grunt, placed the painted music box between his knees and began to turn the handle. A piping, jigging tune began. The woman in pink and her long, thin partner began to dance, their feet thumping on the rough boards. She laughed. He remained as solemn as the grave. The two other men went back to their card game. The young woman in the purple cloak twirled her parasol and stared out at the river.

The companions sat down on a bench by the rail.

"A strange group," Barda muttered. "We will have to keep our wits about us."

"Indeed."

They all looked up. The young woman in purple had moved closer to them. She was still staring at the water, but plainly it was she who had spoken.

Lief stared at her. At the proud tilt of her head,

the painted lips, the black-shadowed eyes, the long golden earrings. Then he had the shock of his life as he recognized her.

It was Jasmine.

✳

The sun was very low in the sky. The *River Queen* chugged on, steadily moving down the river. Lockie the Stripe had at last grown tired of turning the handle of his music box, and was lying flat on his back on the deck with his eyes closed. The woman in pink and her companion were murmuring together. The two card-playing men had begun another game.

Without making any sign that she knew them, Jasmine had moved away from Barda, Lief, and Dain once more. Now she was sitting alone under her parasol at the other end of the boat. "I cannot believe I did not recognize her!" Lief whispered for the twentieth time. "How did she come by those clothes?"

"From our friend Steven, I have no doubt," Barda whispered back. "She must have tried to go inland, to avoid the reed beds, and been forced at last to double back to the Broad River path. So it was that she ended up behind us, instead of in front."

"She is very clever," Dain murmured admiringly, watching Jasmine daintily nibbling dried fruit from a small bag in her hand. "Who would describe her as 'a wild girl' now? But where is her bird?"

Lief glanced at the riverbank, and caught a

glimpse of a black shadow skimming silently through the reeds. Kree was keeping them well in sight.

※

As the sun set, the reed beds at last gave way to flat drifts of sand scattered with low bushes. The moon rose, only to be covered by cloud almost at once. The whistle blew. The *River Queen* slowed and stopped.

"We start again at first light," the captain announced as Chett threw out the anchor with a rattle of chain. "Make yourselves comfortable, friends, and get some rest. But be on guard. Remember, your safety is your business, not mine."

He stumped back into his cabin and shut the door. Everyone heard the firm click as a bolt slid home. Now there was silence, except for the lapping of the water and the creaking of timbers.

Chett ran around the deck, lighting lanterns, but they did little to pierce the darkness beyond the boat. The woman in pink leaned against her companion and closed her eyes. The men at the table threw down their cards, pulled blankets out of their packs, and settled themselves to rest.

Lief, Barda, and Dain ate a little, and drank sparingly. Then they, too, took out blankets, for the night was growing chilly. Lief yawned. The rocking of the boat was making him sleepy. He fought to stay awake.

"I will keep first watch, Lief," said Barda's voice out of the gloom. "Sleep, but be ready. I fear that this is going to be a long night."

11 – In the Night

A shriek woke Lief. He was on his feet in an instant, his hand on his sword. He had no idea how much time had passed. It was very dark. The lanterns had gone out. The sky was black.

"Barda!" he hissed. "Dain!"

The two voices answered close beside him. His companions were also standing and alert.

The shriek came again. Lief realized that it was Kree. Kree was crying a warning. Where was Jasmine? He wanted to call to her, but knew he could not. No one must guess they knew one another.

Sleepy, grumbling voices could be heard around the deck as the other passengers stirred. "It is only a bird, my love," the woman in pink mumbled. "Go back to sleep."

For a moment, there was silence once more, except for the lapping of the water, the creaking of the boat's timbers. But surely — Lief's ears strained — surely the sounds were not quite as they had been before. They were louder. And a slight, bumping noise had joined them.

Another boat . . .

The thought had barely crossed Lief's mind when all of a sudden the darkness around the deck rails seemed to move and thicken. He could hear heavy breathing, and the tinny rattle of steel. The boat was being boarded!

"Beware!" he shouted. "Defend your — "

There was a roar of anger and a rush of feet. Someone cannoned into him, throwing him down violently. He hit the deck with a thump, striking his brow on the corner of something that chimed and jingled. The music box, he thought confusedly. He touched his forehead and felt trickling blood.

Dizzy and sick, he crawled to his knees. Lockie the Stripe was squealing in panic. The woman in pink was screaming and crying. Sounds of fighting filled the darkness. Lief could hear crashes and groans, a bloodcurdling yell, the splash of something heavy falling over the side. He could hear the clash of steel against steel.

"Give us some light, you fool!" roared a voice.

One by one, the lanterns began to glow once more. The polypan was lighting them, grinning and chewing as he swung from one to the other. Gradually, a scene of horror was revealed.

There must have been twenty invaders at least. Men, and women, too, with knives, swords, and axes. They wore a strange array of fine and tattered clothes, their wild hair was matted, their eyes glittering.

Barda, his back against the deck railing, fought two of them. Dain was beside him, fending off a third. Lockie was cringing on the deck. The woman in pink, wailing helplessly, was clutching at the thin man who was shaking her off, crawling away like a long-legged spider looking for a hole to hide in. One of the card-playing men lay dead in a pool of blood. The other had disappeared. Over the side, no doubt, thought Lief, remembering the splash.

Of the captain there was no sign. No doubt he was still locked in his cabin, and Lief was quite sure that he would not venture out for the sake of a few passengers. They had accepted his terms, paid their money, and taken their chances. He had not spent a lifetime on this dangerous river for nothing.

Lief staggered to his feet, feeling for his sword. He had to help Barda. But the deck seemed to be spinning. He could not move fast enough. With horror he saw one of Barda's opponents close in, grabbing a lantern and swinging it in Barda's face. Barda thrust himself backward to escape the flame. The deck rail groaned and began to split.

"No!" cried Lief, lurching forward. But the next second the whole section of deck rail broke away. Barda, the pirate, and the lantern tumbled into the water. There was a tremendous splashing and bubbling. Then silence.

"Barda!" shrieked Lief, stumbling to the gap. But no head broke the surface of the water. The lantern had gone out. All was darkness.

Lief prepared to jump. All he knew was that he had to save Barda, who was somewhere down in that black water. But with despair he felt himself pulled backwards by grasping hands and thrown to the deck again.

"Not until we have picked you clean, boy!" laughed the man above him, a man with a nose that reached almost to his chin, and teeth filed sharp as knives. "The worms can have you then!"

Everything was blurry. Stabs of pain shot through Lief's head as he was rolled and pushed on the deck. The cloak was ripped from his back. His sword and money bag were taken. The embroidered band was pulled from his waist.

No!

He moaned, scrambling to rise. A heavy boot kicked him in the ribs.

"Finish him off, Finn, and the other one, too," screamed a voice.

Finn. Lief squirmed at the sound of the name — one of the names on the walls of Where Waters Meet.

"The other one is valuable," a deeper voice called. "He is with the Resistance. I have seen him with Doom. The Guards will pay in gold for him, alive."

"See what I have found, trying to creep up on us!" A huge, grinning woman with streaming red hair came around the corner of the cabin, hauling Jasmine in her brawny arms. Jasmine's feet were swinging high off the ground. She was kicking and struggling, biting at the hands that gripped her, but the woman took no notice.

"Fine clothes for a fine lady!" she roared. "Would I not look beautiful in these?" She tore off the purple scarf, and Jasmine's tangled black hair swung free. Then the woman set about tearing at the golden cords that bound the cloak around Jasmine's throat.

There was a screech, and a black shadow swooped at her head. With a snap, a sharp beak struck her just above the ear. The woman shrieked and staggered and her grip on Jasmine loosened.

In a flash, Jasmine had wriggled free, leaving her cloak in the woman's hands. In a moment her dagger was in her hand, and her booted foot was kicking backwards with deadly force.

The woman howled and fell back, lurching into Lief's attacker and sending him sprawling. Jasmine hauled Lief to his feet and passed him her second dagger. "Stay behind me!" she ordered. "Where is Barda?"

"Gone," muttered Lief. Jasmine's eyes darkened. As Kree flew down to her arm she whirled to face the pirates, baring her teeth.

Lief saw them hesitate. And well they might. The

78

elegant lady they had thought to rob so easily had become before their eyes a fiery warrior whose dagger glinted as brightly as their swords. Even the polypan was gaping in astonishment. And the woman in pink —

Her mouth was open. Her eyes were burning, huge, fixed on Jasmine. And as she stared, something began to happen to her face. It was as though the burning eyes were melting it. The flesh was paling. The pink curls were shrivelling and drawing back, back to her swelling skull to reveal the mark high on her brow. Her arms and shoulders were bubbling and twisting. Then her whole body was writhing upward, flickering like cold white flame.

"Ol!" The cry of terror echoed around the deck. And instantly the pirates were scattering, scrambling for the rail, dragging Dain and all their booty with them. Their feet crashed onto the deck of their own boat. The polypan leaped after them, chattering and spitting in fear. Oars rattled and splashed as ruffians bent to pull away from the danger, to escape downstream.

But the Ol cared nothing for them. The burning eyes were fixed on Jasmine. The toothless mouth was grinning greedily. It lunged forward, its long, white fingers twitching as they reached for Jasmine's throat.

12 - Shadows

The chill of the Ol came before it — a breathtaking cold that froze the limbs, stung the eyes, and turned the lips to ice. Gasping, staggering back, trying to shield Lief with her body, Jasmine swung her dagger at the white, grasping fingers. Half-stunned with cold, Kree dashed himself against the thing's peaked head.

But nothing, nothing could stop it. The fingers of one hand snaked forward and caught Jasmine around the neck, lifting her from the ground. Almost carelessly, the other hand grasped Lief's dagger arm in a grip of frozen iron. The dagger fell clattering to the deck.

The moon slipped from behind the clouds. Its cool white light flooded the deck, fell over Lief's face. We are dying, he thought, almost in wonder. Time seemed to be moving very slowly.

Then the Ol jerked violently. In a dream of terror, Lief looked up at the vast, wavering body and saw something sharp and gleaming slide out of the right side of its chest, growing longer, longer . . .

The grip on his arm loosened. He saw Jasmine fall. The Ol began to tip forward.

"Get out of the way, you fool!" roared a voice.

Desperately Lief rolled to one side. The Ol crashed to the deck, the wooden pole of the long spike that had pierced its heart sticking up from its back. Its flesh bulged and heaved. Pink curls and a single blue eye bubbled hideously in the whiteness.

Grinning savagely, the captain heaved the spike free and kicked the collapsing body into the river. "Ols! I hate 'em!" he growled.

Lief crawled to Jasmine. Filli was chattering to her, trying to make her open her eyes. She was breathing, but her neck flamed red, as though it had been burned.

Dain's pack was still lying on the deck. Lief tore it open and pulled out the honey jar. He smeared some of the golden stuff on Jasmine's mouth. "Lick your lips, Jasmine," he whispered. "The honey will help you, as it helped Barda." As he said the name, his throat closed with pain.

The captain was looking around, shaking his head. The deck was littered with pirates' bodies. "Looks like your dad dealt with a few of the scum before he went over the side," he said. "They got your brother, too, did they? If he *was* your brother, which I doubt."

Lief swallowed. "They took Dain away," he managed to say. "I have to follow them. Get him back."

And the Belt. The Belt!

The words screamed in his mind and again the dreadfulness of what had happened swept over him.

The captain came closer and peered curiously at Jasmine. Filli hissed and bared his tiny teeth, his fur bristling. The captain jumped back and fell onto a pile of planks. There was a shriek, and Lockie the Stripe crawled out of hiding.

"I can't stand this river," he moaned. "Never again! I'm going to retire. I don't care if I starve!"

"That's what you always say, you cowardly blob!" snarled the captain rudely. "What about my deck rail? And my polypan? Who's going to pay for them?"

"Who cares for that?" cried Lief. "How can you talk of money when the decks are awash with blood?" Angry tears had sprung, scalding, into his eyes.

The captain turned to him, sneering. "If that's how you feel, you can get off, boyo!" he growled. "You, your wildcat friend, *and* her crazy bird. I'll be glad to see the last of you. Don't you think I know why that Ol attacked? It recognized her, didn't it? It had orders to get her. And you, too, for all I know."

He turned, snarling, to Lockie the Stripe. "Row

them to the bank," he snapped. "Get them out of my sight! We're going back to Broad River for repairs."

✳

By the time Lockie, very downcast, had dumped Jasmine and Lief and rowed back to the *River Queen*, steam was already pouring from the boat's funnel. Moments later, the anchor chain clattered and the paddle wheel began to move. The boat turned and chugged away upstream, leaving the companions with only Dain's pack and one blanket for comfort.

Jasmine was conscious, but could barely speak. She took another spoonful of honey and swallowed painfully. "What are we to do?" she croaked.

"Follow the pirates and get the Belt back," muttered Lief, with more confidence than he felt.

Jasmine nodded, her head bowed. "They have Dain, as well as the Belt," she said. "We must help Dain. Barda would have wanted us to do that."

She was shaking all over. Lief took the blanket and wrapped it around her. Then he sat close beside her, for warmth.

"If only we knew where the pirates planned to go!" he said. "The water from the Dreaming Spring would have helped us find out. But all that remains was in the packs." He looked up at the sky. The stars were fading. The pirates' boat must already be far distant.

"We must go," said Jasmine. "They are getting away!" She struggled to rise, but fell back almost at once. Lief covered her again with the blanket. His head was thumping.

"Barda would say that we should rest," he said. "He would say, 'What point is there in catching up to our enemies but being too weak to fight them?' And he would be right. He was almost always right."

"I am glad to hear you say so," growled a familiar voice.

And out of the shadows walked Barda — soaked, shivering, but alive! The shock was so great that for a moment Lief could not speak. But his joy and relief must have shown in his face, for Barda grinned and clapped him on the shoulder as he sat down with a weary groan.

"Did you think I was gone for good?" he asked. "Well, so did I, I confess. But I managed to fight off the cutthroat who went over the side with me. And the worms, if worms there are, must have been busy with other prey."

"The card-playing man," Jasmine suggested huskily. She put her hand to her throat as she spoke, but plainly her pain was already easing, thanks to the Queen Bee honey. And her spirits had soared now that Barda had returned.

Barda nodded gravely. "Perhaps so. I remember little of getting to the bank. I came to myself only a few minutes ago. There was the sound of the boat. Then I heard your voices along the bank."

"Barda, they took the Belt." It was agony for Lief

to say it. "My sword, all our belongings — and Dain."

Barda took a deep breath. "So," he said finally. "So we must deal with that."

He crawled to his feet. "But first we must warm and dry ourselves. We will start a fire — a fine blaze. And if any more enemies see it and come to attack us, they are welcome. A gang of pirates and an Ol together could not finish us — let others try if they dare!"

Lief staggered up and went to help collect wood. The terrible despair that had engulfed him had lifted with Barda's return. But as he plodded the barren sand, now slowly lightening with the coming of dawn, he still felt sick at heart.

It was all very well to speak bravely of following the pirates, of tracking them down. But by the time the companions reached the coast, the battered boat would certainly be hidden away in some sheltered bay. However were they to find it?

He saw some old planks that had washed up on the shore, and walked towards them. Then he realized that there was something else lying in shallow water just beyond the wood. It looked like a heap of rubbish and rags, but it was not. It was a dead man.

"Barda!" he called.

Barda came quickly, and together they pulled the body up onto the sand. "This is the pirate who went into the water with me," Barda said. "He, it seems, was not as lucky as I was."

Lief stared down at the gaunt face. In death, the pirate looked more pathetic than savage. He watched as Barda crouched beside the body and began pulling at the clothing, checking the pockets for weapons or anything else of value. There had been a time when neither of them would have dreamed of robbing a dead body. But that time had long gone.

Barda exclaimed and sat back on his heels. He was holding something in his hand — a thin package wrapped in oilskin. Carefully he unwrapped it. The paper inside was damp, but still in one piece. He placed it on the sand and Lief bent over it. Even in the dim dawn light, he could see clearly what it was.

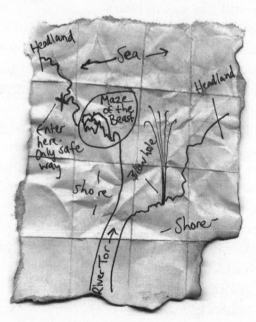

"It is the way to the Maze of the Beast," muttered Barda.

"The pirates are going to the Maze? But why? It is a place of terror." Lief's heart was thudding painfully.

"They would not care, if they had heard of a great gem hidden there." Barda gritted his teeth. "And somehow they have heard of it, Lief. They are going to seek it. And now they have the Belt to help them."

13 ~ Disaster

Two days later the companions stood on the shore, looking out at the vast, foam-flecked blue of the sea. Wind tore at their clothes and whipped their hair. During their cold, hungry journey they had seen several walled villages on the other side of the river, and even passed a bridge. But of the pirates there had been no sign, and even now their boat was nowhere to be seen.

To Jasmine, who had never seen the sea, the ocean was a fresh sight, and a source of wonder. To Lief, at first, it was like a breath of home. Not so much the sight, for the Shadow Lord had long forbidden the coast to the people of Del. But the sound and smell, and the taste of salt on his lips, were achingly familiar.

Yet after only a few moments the feeling melted away and a kind of loathing took its place.

This was not the coast of Del. This coast was bare

and completely silent except for the wind and the pounding waves. There was no sign of any living thing. There were no fish jumping in the swelling water, or crabs scuttling on the sand. And Kree was the only bird in sight.

Lief found himself shrinking from the hissing foam that crawled towards his feet. Into this sea poured all the filth of the River Tor. Its clean, sparkling surface was a lie, for beneath it rolled all the waste and evil the river had been forced to carry for so long. Killer worms squirmed in its depths, feeding on the bodies of the dead, crawling on the wreckage of broken boats. And at the end of the long strip of sand to Lief's left, under the headland that looked like a haggard face, was the place called the Maze of the Beast.

Abruptly Lief turned his head away so that he looked back across the river mouth to his right. Beyond the swirling water, more sand stretched away to another gloomy headland that rose from a base of flat, smooth rock. As he watched, a towering jet of spray spurted into the air from the rock. It was as though some giant creature hidden there was spitting a huge mouthful of water at the sky.

Jasmine hissed with shock.

"Do not fear," muttered Lief. "It is a blowhole. My mother has told me of such things. Water forces its way through a tunnel under the rock, then sprays up through a hole far from where it entered."

"I was not afraid," said Jasmine hastily. "Only

surprised — for a moment. But I am glad we do not have to go to that side."

This side does not hold much joy for us, either, thought Lief, as he began to trudge with his companions along the wet sand. Wind rushed around his ears. The shore ahead was bare, the headland threatening.

He, Barda, and Jasmine had been so careful, for so long. They had borne separation, they had crept and hidden. But here, where the Shadow Lord's servants must surely be watching and waiting, they had no choice but to show themselves.

There was nowhere to hide. And they no longer had the Belt to warn them of approaching peril.

Lief glanced at Barda and felt the same pang of dismay that he had felt many times over the past two days. The big man was walking with bowed head, as though he had forgotten that danger might at any time swoop at them from the skies or rise from beneath the sand. He was meekly following Jasmine, who was striding ahead, her eyes darting everywhere.

The unexpected finding of the pirates' map, which had given Lief and Jasmine a new burst of energy, seemed to have made Barda thoughtful and withdrawn. Except to urge haste, he had said little as they moved on down the river. While his companions talked of their hopes and fears, he simply listened.

Plainly, he had something on his mind. Something he would not share. When Lief took risks, he did not complain. When Jasmine stopped to pick up bits and pieces washed up on the riverbank, he said nothing. He was so patient and gentle, in fact, that Lief became uncomfortable, and longed to hear the old, irritable Barda growling once more.

Jasmine glanced behind her, and Lief saw her forehead crease in a frown as she noticed Barda's downcast head. Lief ran to catch up with her.

"Could he be ill?" she whispered. "Or has he simply lost heart?"

Lief shook his head. "Things have been desperate before, and always he has been a tower of strength. This is different. Perhaps — perhaps he senses the coming of some great disaster."

This time it was his turn to look sideways at his companion. And, as he had feared she might, Jasmine snorted and tossed her head. "Barda does not have magic powers! He cannot see into the future! And even if he could, what greater disaster could there be than what has happened already?"

She looked ahead again, her face grim. They had nearly reached the rocks. Calling Kree to her, she hunched her shoulders against the cold, waiting for Barda to catch up.

The wind-torn cliff frowned above them. The rocks rose to cruel peaks, then fell away into gaps pitted with dark holes. Waves crashed against them, spattering the companions with spray as they began cautiously to make the slippery crossing. Still there was no sign of the pirates, or of any other enemy.

How strange, thought Lief uneasily. Why . . . ?

Then he saw the cave. It gaped in the cliff face just beyond where he was standing — a dark, secret mouth, above the reach of the waves and hidden from both sides by jagged rocks.

He beckoned to Barda and Jasmine, and silently they all crept to the cave entrance. A cold, dank draught of air sighed into their faces. It was like the breath of the sea — breath tinged with salt and death.

Filli whimpered from his hiding place under Jasmine's jacket. She put up a hand to calm him and moved into the dimness.

Lief and Barda quickly followed. Lief blinked, waiting for his eyes to adjust to the dim light. But even before they had done so, he knew that the cave was empty of life. It would be impossible for any place where a living creature breathed to be so utterly still.

Yet his skin still prickled as though danger was threatening. Suddenly he heard Jasmine draw a sharp breath, and Barda give a low groan. He snatched the dagger from his waistband . . .

And then he saw what his companions had seen before him.

A gaping hole yawned in the ground — a hole that led to a ghastly darkness. You could see, by the sand piled around it, that it had been dug very recently. There were heavy boot prints everywhere.

A paper lay half-buried in the sand. Lief picked it up. It was another copy of the pirates' map.

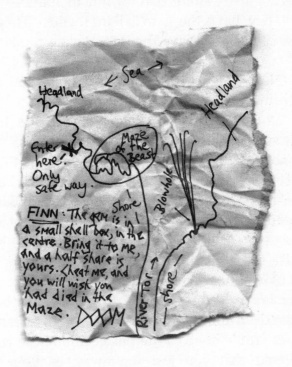

His voice shaking, Lief read the message aloud.

"Doom guessed our goal. Betrayed us!" Jasmine cried.

Lief forced his stiff lips to move. "It may not be too late. Perhaps the pirates did not find the gem. Perhaps the Beast in the Maze killed them."

"I fear that is too much to hope for." Barda had

picked up another object from the sand. It was a small box made of pearl shell. Its hinges had been broken as if rough, greedy hands had torn them apart.

"They have the gem," Barda said. "They have the gem, and they have the Belt. We are too late. It is over."

"No! We must give chase! We must find them!" Lief crumpled the paper in his hand.

"Do not deceive yourself," said Barda heavily. "With such riches in their hands, the pirates would have no need to return to the river. By now they will be far out to sea, putting as much distance between Doom and themselves as possible, and looking for strangers with whom to trade. They are out of our reach."

He put a gentle hand on Lief's shoulder. "It is a bitter blow, but we must face it," he said. "Our quest is over. We must return to Del." He kicked at the tumbled sand. "Think of this, Lief. Now your parents can be freed. You can go to the palace and show yourself — pretend that you just ran away, as your father said."

Our quest is over. Face it. Slowly, Lief nodded. Drearily, he thought of Dain, now beyond help.

Jasmine had been very silent. Lief glanced at her. She was standing on the other side of the cave, utterly still. Kree sat like a carved statue on her arm. Jasmine's face was in shadow, but in her hand something gleamed. Lief went cold.

Jasmine had drawn her dagger. But why? And why was she standing so still? As though she was afraid to move. Afraid to startle . . .

He began to turn. And at once, like a snake striking, someone who had crept up behind him lunged forward. Barda flung up his arms with a bellow of agony as a great sword plunged home, spearing him through the chest.

Lief heard his own cry echoing around the cave. His ears ringing, his heart wrung, he spun around, dagger in hand, ready to leap at the attacker.

And then his jaw dropped. For standing there, panting and haggard, pulling his bloodstained sword from the falling body, was another Barda.

14 - Meetings

Wildly, Lief swung to look at the figure now collapsed on the ground. His stomach heaved as he saw the face dissolving, the body collapsing into a writhing mass. The long, crooked hands of the pink-haired lady's dancing partner pushed out of the whiteness, to be quickly followed by the head of a white water bird and many other eyes and mouths that Lief did not recognize.

"Ol!" he hissed.

"Of course!" Barda's voice rumbled behind him. "How could you have been deceived?"

Hearing that gloriously familiar, irritable growl, Lief dropped the dagger with a cry of joy and flung his arms around Barda's shoulders.

"Steady," said the big man uncomfortably. But he did not pull away.

"When I saw you at the cave entrance, I could not believe it!" Jasmine had bounced over to Barda and was embracing him in her turn. "How did this happen?"

Barda shrugged. "The Ol thought I was dead. But I am not killed so easily. I crawled ashore and took much time to regain strength enough to follow your tracks."

He shook his head. "One set of tracks puzzled me. But when I reached here, I understood." He grimaced with distaste at the remains of the Ol, now just a bubbling pool on the cave floor.

"I should have known!" said Lief. "You — I mean, *it* — spoke of how we had escaped from pirates and an Ol! Yet you had gone over the side, Barda, before the Ol that was the pink-haired woman revealed itself. How could you have known about it?"

"And no wonder it was so quiet and gentle!" Jasmine exclaimed. "It could copy your appearance and voice, and learn about us from what we said. But it did not know how to behave. It had not had time to learn what you were really like!"

Barda raised an eyebrow and Jasmine realized, too late, that her words had not been very flattering. She busied herself picking up the second dagger and tucking it into her boot.

"I may not be particularly quiet and gentle by nature, Jasmine," said Barda dryly. "But on the other hand, I would not have been persuaded to give up our quest because of one small problem."

"One small problem?!" Lief exclaimed. "The pirates have the sixth gem, and the Belt! And they are far away!"

"How do you know they are far away?" Barda demanded. "Because an Ol told you so? The pirates could be sheltering in a bay just around the headland at this very moment, for all you know."

He waved a hand at the hole in the sand. "And if they have found the gem, so much the better. I would prefer to get it from them than face the Beast."

The sickening vision the opal had given him rose in Lief's mind. Suddenly he longed for fresh air. He turned and blundered out of the cave . . .

Straight into the arms of a grinning man whose hooked nose nearly met his chin, whose yellowed teeth were filed to sharp points, and whose savage eyes gleamed with triumph.

✳

There were only two pirates in all, but with a sword pressed against Lief's throat, Barda and Jasmine had no choice but to surrender. Bound cruelly together, the three were hauled back across the rocks and into a rowing boat, with Kree swooping helplessly above them.

"Did I not tell you I saw movement in the cave, Nak?" chattered the man with the filed teeth. "Was it not worth making a landing?"

"They will make fine sport," agreed his companion, the huge red-haired woman who had seized Jasmine on the *River Queen*.

She twisted her fingers in Jasmine's hair and spitefully wrenched the girl's head back, so that she could stare down into her face. "You will learn not to kick your betters, fine lady!" she snarled. "We have a special fate reserved for trespassers on our shore. A little pet we want you to meet. Is that not so, Finn?"

The man sniggered agreement. As he took his place in the boat, he unbuttoned his coat. He was wearing the embroidered belt. He noticed Lief's eyes upon it, and grinned evilly. "Do you miss it?" he jeered. "I am not surprised. It is heavier than it looks — fine quality indeed! But you will not need it where you are going."

And, still laughing, he bent to the oars.

✳

Once the boat had reached the calmer water beyond the waves, it turned and began to go back the way the companions had come. It reached the place where the Tor joined the sea and moved on, Kree battling the wind overhead, Finn and Nak straining against the current.

At last they drew opposite the blowhole, skirting the sheet of rock with care. And there was the pirate boat, rocking in shallow water, sheltering in an enormous cavern in the headland.

"Do not follow us, Kree!" shrieked Jasmine to the sky. "Wait!"

"If he does, he will wait forever," sneered Nak.

As the rowing boat slid into the cavern, Lief saw the rest of the pirate crew eating and drinking on a huge ledge above the water. The polypan ran to and fro, carrying dishes, ordered about by everyone. There was something different about it, Lief thought. It looked harried and unhappy, but that was not all. He thought about it for a moment, then noticed something else.

Dain lay in a corner, firmly bound. Another prisoner lay with him — a man in a tight blue coat.

Nak and Finn were greeted with cheers. Lief, Barda, and Jasmine were pushed and jeered at for a time, then thrown down with Dain and the other man.

"Their screams will be music to my ears!" screeched Nak, as she swaggered back to the crowd. "But it will be all the sweeter on a full stomach!"

As soon as she had gone, Lief saw Filli slip from Jasmine's jacket and scurry to her boot. With all his might the little creature tried to pull the hidden dagger free, but the task was far beyond his strength.

Dain's exhausted eyes were dark with misery. "I knew that if you were alive, you would come for me," he breathed. "At first I prayed you would — then I prayed you would not. Now what I feared has come to pass. They have you."

"What is to be done with us?" whispered Lief.

Dain licked his lips. "I do not know," he answered. "But they speak of something called the Glus."

The man in the blue coat moaned in terror.

Dain glanced at him. "This is Milne. They call him a traitor. He tried to kill Nak, when she said he was a fool for bringing me with them."

Milne, thought Lief. Milne. Nak. Finn. Well, I hoped to meet the owners of those names, and so I have. If we have to die, at least we will be taking one of them with us.

The polypan had been sniffing around them. Now it pushed its face into Lief's chest and whimpered. Lief tried to push it away. Its smell was horrible. It reminded him of something, but he could not think what.

"Are they still going to give you to the Grey Guards, Dain?" hissed Jasmine.

Dain nodded. "Yes, though there was bitter argument. Milne and the others liked the plan. But Nak and Finn were afraid."

"Afraid?" Lief looked at Nak and Finn laughing around the fire. "They seem to fear nothing."

A strange, baffled expression crossed Dain's face. "They fear Doom," he whispered. "Finn said that if Doom ever finds out that they have knowingly betrayed the Resistance, their lives will not be worth a handful of ash. Doom will hunt them down one by one, and they will never escape him."

Cheat me, and you will wish you had died in the Maze.

So that is why the pirates are still here, thought Lief. They are too afraid to run from Doom.

"We leave tonight," Dain was saying. "Nak and Finn refuse to go. They will stay here with the booty. The rest will sail with me up the river to meet the Guards near Dread Mountain."

The polypan was pawing at Lief again. "What ails you?" he said angrily, trying to squirm away from it. "What do you want from me?"

Then, suddenly, he knew.

15 - The Glus

Lief whispered urgently. The polypan listened. At first it shook its head, then, finally, it nodded and darted away.

Barda and Jasmine took no notice of it. They were concentrating on Dain.

He was biting his lip, plainly still confused and shaken by what he had heard the pirates say. "I thought I knew Doom," he muttered. "Now it seems I knew but little. Finn spoke of him — as though he had powers beyond those of an ordinary man."

"Then Finn is a fool!" Jasmine said decidedly. She raised her chin as they all glanced at her. "I fought Doom in Rithmere, remember," she went on. "I felt his danger then, and understood it. Doom does not care if he lives or dies. Whatever he has suffered has scarred his heart as well as his face. Inside him now there is only anger, bitterness, and cold."

"So he has nothing left to lose," Barda murmured.

Jasmine shivered. "That is what makes him a deadly enemy. That is the source of his power. But it is a power I should not care to have." She put up her hand to fondle Filli's soft fur.

Chett came chattering up and pulled Lief's sleeve impatiently.

"Put it on me, under my shirt," Lief hissed. "Only then . . ."

This time, Jasmine and Barda, and Dain, too, were watching. Lief saw his friends' eyes widen as the polypan, grumbling, fastened the embroidered belt around his waist. He saw them glance wildly at Finn, who was eating and drinking with his companions, quite unaware that he had been robbed.

"You are a fine thief indeed, Chett," said Lief. He rolled on his side and let the polypan take what it wanted from his pocket — the little packet he had bought from Steven. The creature unwrapped the glossy brown stuff, stuck it into its mouth, and began chewing blissfully.

"This gum is a great polypan favorite, it seems," Lief said. "Chett went with the pirates not knowing that they do not keep supplies of it for rewards, as the *River Queen* captain does. Was it not fortunate that I happened to have some?"

Barda wet his lips. "Jasmine has a second dagger

in her boot. Would Chett get it out, in return for another piece for later?" he asked.

The polypan shook its head violently.

"I have already tried that," Lief answered smoothly. "But Chett was afraid to go so far. I said that Nak and Finn would never find out who had done it — "

"Indeed!" Barda and Jasmine agreed together.

But still the polypan shook its head, casting envious eyes at Lief's pockets.

"So then I asked for my belt," said Lief, carefully looking anywhere but at Dain. "It has value for me, Barda, because you gave it to me."

"Of course." Barda nodded. "And the other little treasure? The pretty jewel found only a day or two ago? In a small pearl-shell box?"

"Chett seems never to have heard of it," said Lief. "Finn is keeping it to himself, I think."

"Treasure?" Suddenly interested, Milne rolled over and glared at them with bloodshot eyes. Dain, too, raised himself on one elbow and stared.

Not sure of the wisdom of what he was doing, Lief ploughed on recklessly. "We had a map, but we arrived at the spot too late. Finn had already been there. Wait! I will show you."

He whispered to the polypan. Chewing madly and grinning with delight, it dug its hand into another of his pockets and drew out the map Lief had found on the cave floor. It trotted over and put the map in front of Milne. Then it darted back to Lief. He rolled again so that it could claim its second reward.

Milne squinted at the paper. His lips moved as he made out the words, especially the note on the side — the note signed "Doom." For a brief moment he was silent. Then, with a sneer, he rolled over on his back again and turned his head away.

Before Lief had time to wonder about this, he was pulled roughly to his feet.

"Time to dispose of our garbage!" grinned Finn, shaking him by the collar. The other pirates, flushed with eating and drinking, swarmed over their victims and began dragging them out of the cavern and onto the great expanse of smooth rock that stretched out to sea. Dain, left behind, moaned helplessly, struggling against the ropes that bound him.

"Listen to me!" Lief shouted at the top of his voice. "Finn has cheated you! He has treasure that he has not shared! He found a great gem!"

There was sudden stillness. "Oh?" asked Nak in a hard voice, glancing at Finn. "A great gem? Where did he find it."

"In the Maze of the Beast!" shouted Lief.

To his amazement, the men and women around him, including Nak and Finn, began shrieking with laughter.

"Aha! Then you and your friends can perhaps find another one!" jeered Nak. "No doubt the Glus will be happy to help you look. We will cut your ropes, so you can enjoy yourselves for longer."

There was the sound of stone grating on stone as a huge boulder was pushed away from a round black hole in the rock.

"Good hunting!" snarled Finn. Lief felt his ropes being cut through. The next instant there was a shove in the small of his back. Then he was pitching headfirst into the hole, and down, down, into darkness.

✳

There were many sounds. The sound of Milne sobbing in helpless terror. Faint laughter from above as the stone was shoved back into place. The sound of dripping water echoing, echoing through endless, winding spaces. And something worse. The sticky, stealthy sliding of something huge, stirring.

Lief opened his eyes. He knew what he would see.

Eerie, bluish light. Great dripping spears of stone hanging from the roof. Thick, lumpy pillars rising from the floor. Twisted columns, rippled and grooved, like water made solid. Gleaming, ridged walls, running with milky liquid.

The Maze of the Beast. How could he have thought they would escape it? It had always been their fate.

Lief turned, wincing at the pain in his shoulder. Jasmine and Barda were crawling upright, looking around in dazed confusion. Milne thrashed and wallowed in the water at their feet.

The sliding sound grew louder.

"It is coming," Milne sobbed. "The Glus . . ."

Jasmine snatched her dagger from her boot and swung around, facing first one way, then another. "I cannot tell where it is coming from!" she cried. "It seems all around us. Which way — ?"

The sound of monstrous, sliding flesh was everywhere.

Then they saw it — a gigantic, sluglike beast, sickly pale, oozing towards them. It filled the vast passage through which it crawled, its swollen body rippling horribly, its tiny eyes waving on the ends of stalks at the top of its terrible head.

Gabbling with terror, Milne staggered to his feet.

The Glus lunged forward, rearing its head. Its spine-tipped tail thrashed. Its bloodred mouth yawned wide. Mottled stripes lit up along its back.

A thick, gurgling, sucking sound began, deep in its chest. Then, with terrifying suddenness, a tangle of fine white threads sprayed out of its throat, aimed directly at Milne.

Screaming, Milne dodged, flailing with his arms. Most of the threads fell short of their mark, but a few drifted onto one hand and a shoulder, drawing them together and binding them like ropes of steel. He stumbled and fell, struggling to pull his hand free, rolling and kicking in the water.

"Get up!" screamed Jasmine, plunging towards him, holding out her hand. The Beast thrashed, rearing, the stripes on its back glowing like evil lights, the stalks on its head moving, dipping, as its cold, vacant eyes fixed themselves upon her. Jasmine slashed at it in a useless attempt to keep it back.

The bloodred jaws opened. The thick, gurgling sound began again. Still Jasmine reached out for Milne. Still he screamed and writhed in helpless panic.

"Jasmine, no! You cannot help him!" Barda caught Jasmine around the waist, swinging her back and aside, just as the Beast struck again. White threads cascaded from its throat, covering Milne's head and neck with a stiffening helmet of white.

Half-blinded, mad with terror, Milne floundered to his feet and splashed blindly away, one arm crooked helplessly as he blundered into the depths of the blue-lit maze.

The Glus paused, its eyestalks waving. Then, as the companions stood frozen, staring in fascinated horror, it effortlessly turned its vast body, oozed through a narrow gap between two columns as easily as though it was made of oil, and followed him.

"Now is our chance," said Jasmine urgently. "Quickly! There is fresh air down here. I can smell it. And where there is air, there is a way out!"

"Give me the dagger!" hissed Lief, pulling off the embroidered belt. Wordlessly Jasmine thrust the weapon into his hands. Lief stuck the sharp point into the fabric of the belt and ripped the embroidery apart. The Belt of Deltora slid out into his hands.

For a split second he gazed at it. It was so beautiful. So precious. But the ruby was pale. The emerald was dull.

Danger. Evil. Fear.

"Lief!" shouted Barda.

Lief clasped the Belt around his waist. He gripped it with his hands, drawing strength from its familiar weight and warmth. Perhaps, now, it would never be complete. But even as it was, it had power. The topaz gleamed through his fingers, bright, rich gold.

†   The Topaz is a powerful gem, and its strength increases as the moon grows full . . . It strengthens and clears the mind . . .

The moon was high above them, blocked by churning sea and a mountain of rock, but still its power reached the stone. Lief felt his mind clear and sharpen, as the mists of confusion and fear lifted.

"This way!" he shouted, pointing to a passage that led away from where Milne had gone. "But slowly, carefully. I think the Beast's eyes and hearing are weak, but it is attracted by movement. It feels movement in the Maze, as a spider feels insects struggling in its web. That is why it chased Milne, instead of staying and attacking us."

It was agony to move slowly, when every instinct was telling them to run, run blindly as Milne had done. They crept along, through passage after passage, twisting and turning. They wet their hands and their faces, the better to feel that breath of coolness that would warn them of a crack, a gap, a way out.

16 ~ Discoveries

At last they could walk no farther. They squeezed into a narrow space between two lumpy, dripping walls. There they rested, panting and shivering, one wall pressed hard against their backs, the other a hand's breadth from their faces. The sound of Milne's screams and splashes floated, echoing, in the air. He was still running, lost somewhere in the Maze.

And the terrible sound of the Glus never stopped.

"It is moving so slowly," whispered Jasmine, listening. "How can it hope to catch him?"

"It has only to follow, and wait," said Barda. "Even if he does not make a mistake, and meets it face to face around some corner, he will have to rest sooner or later."

His voice sounded odd. Lief glanced at him

quickly. Barda was looking at the wall in front of him. Carefully he raised his hand and slowly traced shapes in the gleaming stone.

A bony arm. Five fingers. A skull, its mouth gaping in a silent scream.

"Here is one who stopped to rest, and stopped too long," Barda said. He twisted his neck and looked over his shoulder. Milky drops ran slowly, ceaselessly down the wall at his back. Already they were pooling on his shoulders, setting into a fine crust of stone.

With a cry of horror, Lief and Jasmine pulled themselves forward. Drying stone cracked and slid from their backs and shoulders, splashing into the water at their feet. They edged out of their hiding place and, looking back, saw their own shapes imprinted in the wall.

"How long would it have taken before we were stuck fast?" asked Barda grimly. "An hour, perhaps? Even less? If we had slept . . ."

They began to move again. And now they saw the twisted shapes, the lumps and ridges on walls, columns, and pillars, for what they were. Everywhere they looked were the bones of the dead — clawing hands, sprawled legs, skulls that seemed to shriek of terror.

Lief felt himself shivering all over. He imagined the horror of waking and finding himself trapped by the stone of the wall. He imagined struggling, struggling . . . while the Glus moved slowly towards him.

"We must not rest," he muttered. "We must not sleep."

They crept on, and on, trying to make as little movement as possible, their faces turned to the wall, their hands held out in front of them. After a while, Lief's thoughts became a wandering haze — a haze of water, white walls, endless movement, words. *There is a way out. We must find it. We must not rest. We must not sleep.*

✳

Lief's head fell forward, jolting him awake. He blinked, confused, and realized that he had been walking in a dream. He had no idea of how much time had passed.

Dimly, he became aware that Milne's screams and splashes had stopped. Perhaps they had stopped a long time ago.

And if — if Milne had stopped running, where was the Beast? Sweat breaking out on his brow, Lief listened to the echoes, and at last made out a soft, horrible sound, mingling with the dripping water. It was not the sticky sliding he had heard before, but a still, sighing, sucking sound that raised the hairs on the back of his neck.

"Barda, Jasmine . . ." he whispered. But his friends did not answer. They moved, but their eyes were fixed and glazed. They were in a dreamlike state, as he had been.

He took a breath to speak again. Then, suddenly, it was as though a flame shot through him, from his fingers to his face.

The Belt! The Belt had grown hot! Lief stopped, shocked and disbelieving. A rounded pillar of stone stood beside him. Cautiously he moved towards it. The Belt grew even hotter. It seemed to burn under his fingers.

Barda and Jasmine were turning a corner, moving out of sight. Calling, he splashed forward recklessly, catching at their arms to stop them.

Then he froze. For straight ahead of them was the Glus. Its bloated body was rippling and heaving, its head invisible. And from the billowing mountain of flesh came that soft, hideous sound.

But in the same moment, the sound stopped. The body stilled, the head reared upright and faced them, its gaping mouth dripping with blood. The Glus slithered forward, away from the ghastly remains of Milne on which it had been feasting, towards the new disturbance. Its spiked tail curved upward. The stripes on its back began to glow.

Then it struck, lunging forward, white threads hissing from its throat.

Lief, Jasmine, and Barda hurled themselves backwards, falling into the water, scrambling up again and plunging away. The Glus moved on, a little faster.

They reached the rounded pillar of stone. Lief

caught hold of it, the Belt burning at his waist. "Barda, Jasmine, the gem is here, inside the stone!" he shouted.

Barda and Jasmine swung around, disbelieving. He nodded violently. "We have been deceived. The gem has been here, all the time."

"Lief — leave it! We must run!" Jasmine urged, tugging his arm, her eyes on the Glus, swollen and ghastly, sound bubbling deep in its chest.

"No!" Lief cried, holding fast to the pillar. "If I leave this place now I will never find it again!"

"If you stay you will die!" Jasmine shrieked. "Lief!"

Barda gripped her shoulder. His face was grim and set. "Jasmine and I will draw the Beast away, Lief," he snapped. "Stay still — still as that stone — until we are long gone. Then get the gem and do your best to find your way out. Jasmine! Your dagger!"

"No! We must stay together!" Lief shouted, as Jasmine passed him the weapon.

But already Barda was pulling Jasmine away. She was fumbling inside her jacket. At last she pulled out a ball of yellow wool. Shaking off Barda's hand, she plunged back to Lief's side, pulling out a trail of wool as she ran.

"I found this in Where Waters Meet. Hold it fast!" she cried, thrusting the loose end of the wool into Lief's hand. "It will be our line back to you."

"Beware!" Barda roared.

Lief slid behind the stone. Jasmine leaped away. Another tangle of white threads sprayed towards them, falling into the water just short of its mark. Jasmine turned and ran, splashing, back to Barda, leaving a trail of wool behind her. Shoulder to shoulder they waded on till they were lost in the maze.

Then there was only the lapping of the water, the dripping from the roof and the stealthy slithering of the Glus as slowly, slowly, it followed.

Lief crouched, holding his breath, as it passed him, its tiny eyes waving at the ends of their fleshy stalks. Its body narrowed, then bulged horribly, as it squeezed past the stone. Now he saw that its skin was covered in short, fine hairs that stuck straight out, quivering, alive to every ripple, every splash, every tiny movement in the waters of its kingdom. One mistake, and it would be upon him.

Still. Still as the stone.

The Beast crawled on. Every muscle in Lief's body was twitching, aching to move. But he held himself rigid, the slender yellow thread that was his link to Barda and Jasmine clutched tightly in his hand.

✳

Cautiously, Lief stood up. The Glus was long gone. He could hear it moving, far away. But he could no longer hear the splashing sounds of Barda and Jasmine running. They were remaining still — to confuse it, perhaps, or simply to rest. In any case, they led it away from him. They had done their part. Now he could do his.

To what purpose, Lief? a voice inside him seemed to mock. With the gem, or without it, you will walk this maze till you can walk no farther. Then the Glus will bind you with its sticky threads, and suck the flesh from your bones. What it did to Milne, it will do to you.

Lief shut the voice out of his mind. He put one hand on the Belt of Deltora, and the other on the pillar of stone. He moved his fingers over the cool, wet surface, waiting, waiting . . .

And then he felt it. The unmistakable throb that told him where the gem lay. About two-thirds of the way up the pillar.

He began to dig with the point of the dagger, holding his free hand cupped beneath it to catch falling fragments. The outer layer of the stone was soft and damp. It came away easily, and soon he had made a hole big enough to take his whole hand. But as he came to the center of the pillar, the work was more difficult. The sharp steel grated against the harder stone, setting his teeth on edge. Always he was terrified that if he worked too fast, too carelessly, he would injure the gem.

He could see nothing within the hole. He could hear nothing. He could smell nothing. So, he thought, all that is left is touch. I must be like the Glus, and let touch guide me.

He closed his eyes. He moved his hand down the dagger till the point was as one with his fingertips. He scraped delicately, calling the smothered gem in his mind, probing at the same time with his fingers for the touch that would tell him . . .

And there it was. A cool, still center within the column. The moment his fingers touched it, the coolness rolled forward into his hand, the white stone around it crumbling to powder.

Slowly, carefully he withdrew his hand and uncurled his fingers. There, veiled by a film of white dust, was a great purple gem.

The amethyst, symbol of truth.

A feeling of immense peace stole over Lief as he smoothed the dust from its shining surface, marvelling at its beauty. The Belt around his waist was burning hot, but his mind was cool and clear. He remembered words about the amethyst in *The Belt of Deltora*:

✝ **The amethyst, symbol of truth, calms and soothes . . .**

Indeed, Lief thought. And calm is what I need now. The calm to place this gem into the Belt, where it will be safe. The calm to wait until Jasmine and Barda return to me. The calm to believe that they *will* return.

He crouched, water swimming about him. He unclipped the Belt of Deltora and placed it across his knees. The amethyst slid into place beside the emerald and shone there steadily. Lief replaced the Belt around his waist, and carefully stood up again.

Now, I have only to wait, he told himself. He raised his wet hands to dry them on his shirt. And it was then that he felt it, cool on the back of his left hand: a soft breath of air, coming from behind him.

17 - Fight for Freedom

L ief turned. Slowly, slowly. Holding his hand in front of him, guided by the draught of air, he moved to the wall that loomed on the other side of the stone pillar.

There was a small gap at the top. A gap that could have been a fold in the stone, but was not. Through that gap, fresh, salty air streamed. Now he could not only feel it, but smell it.

He lifted Jasmine's dagger and chipped at the place. Soft stone fell into his other hand. There was the gentle whistling of a breeze. Forcing himself to be patient, he gently lowered the loose stone onto the ground at his feet. He rose and chipped again. This time a larger piece of stone came loose. Now the gap was large. Now the air was blowing into his face, and the hollow sound of rushing water was mingling with the sound of the breeze.

Lief's chest was tight. He was panting. He put his hand to the amethyst, to calm himself. It was vital, vital that he did not hurry or panic. He put down the large piece of stone, as gently as he had the first. He took another chip of rock. And another.

And that last was one too many. Water began trickling from the gap. The tunnel that was beyond the wall was half full of water. And Lief had chipped too far.

Almost with despair, he saw the trickling stream hit the water at his feet. The splashing sound seemed loud — impossibly loud. The water swirled and rippled. There was nothing he could do to stop it. As if his mind had eyes, he saw the quivering hairs on the skin of the Glus stiffen. He saw the Glus begin to turn, rearing its head. He saw it moving. Moving towards him.

He heard running, far away, coming closer. At the same moment, the yellow wool tied to his wrist tightened. He forced himself to wait, to watch.

"Lief!" the call burst out of the blue-white shadows. "Lief, what is happening? Lief, it is coming!"

Barda and Jasmine were running towards him, following the yellow thread.

Lief waited no longer. He jumped, heaving himself up into the gap in the wall, gasping as icy water rose, slapping, to his waist. There was rock beneath his feet, and above his head. But it was not the rock of the cave. It was much harder and darker. And the water was not milky, but clear, and sharp with salt.

He leaned down, holding out his arms to Jasmine. As she reached him, he swung her up beside him.

Then it was Barda's turn. He grabbed the edge of the gap. The stone crumbled under his hands and he fell back, gasping as salty water poured over him.

"Barda!" screamed Jasmine.

For the Glus was coming. It was coming, not slowly, but with tremendous speed. The sound of it was ghastly. Its mouth gaped in a snarl, a red gash in the whiteness. White threads sprayed into the air before it like a cloud.

Lief and Jasmine bent forward, muscles straining, hauling Barda upward through the pouring water. Barda's legs kicked frantically, his feet scrabbling for footholds.

He clambered into the tunnel, drawing up his feet just as a shower of threads clamped to the wall below him. He crawled, gasping, clear of the gap. The terrible head of the Glus reared up, filling the space.

"It is coming after us!" Jasmine shrieked.

But the Glus made no attempt to enter the tunnel. Instead, the head began to wag from side to side. White threads poured from the red throat, clinging and sticking to the edges of the gap. And then they realized what was happening.

The Glus was sealing the hole. The danger to the Maze, the vast lair it had built itself over the centuries, was more important than food.

"What is this place?" Jasmine's teeth were chattering. She screamed as the water in the tunnel suddenly surged, knocking her over, tumbling her forward. She came up gasping and choking, Filli squealing. Swept off his own feet by the current, Lief grabbed for her hand.

"We must be under the rock in front of the pirates' cave," shouted Barda, shaking water from his hair and eyes. "The tide is coming in. Hold on!"

With both hands he braced himself against the rock as the water was sucked back, rushing past them, gurgling like water in a drain. Gritting his teeth, Lief clung to Jasmine's hand, stopping her from being swept helplessly backwards.

"Move forward!" Barda roared. "And when the next wave comes, go with it! Do not fight it!"

Again the water swelled and surged. Again they were swept helplessly forward, their bodies tumbled against smooth walls. Again they spluttered to the surface. Again they braced themselves against the rock as the water sucked back.

"The waves are growing bigger! They will fill the tunnel! We will drown!" screamed Jasmine.

Lief tightened his grip on her hand. "We will not!" he shouted. "We have not come so far to die now."

"There!" Barda shouted.

Lief looked ahead, and saw light.

"It is the blowhole!" Desperately, Barda pushed Lief and Jasmine forward. "Go! Quickly! It is almost ready to blow. We must get out before it does. We must!"

Lief remembered the towering spout, the water crashing back to the unforgiving rocks, then sucking back with a force no one could resist. He struggled on, half-crawling, half-swimming, Jasmine sobbing and scrambling ahead of him.

The surge of a new wave overcame him, sealing his eyes, filling his ears with its roaring. Is this the one? The one that will mean our death? he thought, as he was swept towards the light. But still he gripped Jasmine's hand, and when he opened his stinging eyes there was sky above their heads. Dawn sky. They were bobbing in the mouth of the blowhole.

Lief pushed Jasmine up, up and out. She flopped onto the wet rock as he clambered after her, fighting against the water as it sought to pull him back into the tunnel. Barda followed, panting and dripping, taking great gasps of air.

Between them they hauled Jasmine to her feet and began floundering away from the hole, making for the shore.

There was a glad screech as Kree swooped towards them. Then there was a shout from behind. Lief looked back. Two figures were running from the pirates' cave, pounding across the sheet of rock towards them.

Finn and Nak, swords held high, howling in fury.

We have only one dagger, Lief thought, running, the breath rasping in his throat. One dagger against two swords . . .

There was a soft rumbling sound.

"Jump!" Barda roared.

Lief jumped. His feet hit the sand of the shore. He rolled over, breathless, Jasmine and Barda tumbling beside him. He looked back at the rock.

Nak and Finn had stopped. It was as if they were frozen in mid-stride. Their faces were masks of terror. Then, terribly slowly it seemed, they began to turn, casting away the swords, taking one step, another . . .

Too late. The blowhole gushed, roaring, throwing them onto their backs. They scrambled helplessly for a moment, like overturned crabs. Then with a mighty crash the water fell back on them, swirling them, catching them in its grip. With a terrible sucking sound it began to rush, rush back into its rocky tunnel.

Then it was gone, and there was nothing but smooth, wet rock, and two swords lying in puddles of water that gleamed in the rising sun.

✳

The companions gathered their possessions from the deserted pirates' cave, then turned their backs upon the surging waves of the shore. Exhausted and hungry as they were, they wanted nothing more than to put as much distance as possible between themselves and that terrible sea.

The sun was high in the sky when finally they found a place where they could feel safe — a long-abandoned hut by the riverside. They made a fire in the crumbling fireplace, for comfort and warmth. Then, ravenously, they ate nuts and dried fruit, traveller's biscuits, and Queen Bee honey, washed down with water from the crystal streams of Dread Mountain.

They talked little at first. None of them wanted to think of what they had seen, what they had survived. Lief's thoughts drifted to Dain. Would he live to make his way to Tora? Would they meet again? And what of Doom . . . ?

Jasmine spoke at last, echoing his thoughts strangely. "Did Doom betray us?" she murmured. "Or was the writing forged, to make us suspect him?"

Lief shook his head helplessly. He did not know.

"The map was all a lie. A false clue," Jasmine persisted.

"Planted on the dead pirate by that Ol in my shape, to lead you astray and at last cause you to abandon the quest!" Barda shook his head in disgust. "No doubt there were a hundred copies, and a hundred Ols on the river to carry them. Ols with orders to deceive, rather than to kill, if they found us."

Jasmine shuddered. "This was why no enemies waited for us on the shore. The plan this time was to cause us to abandon the quest, and to spread the word that it was hopeless, so that it would never be attempted again."

"Ols to kill. Ols to deceive. The Enemy has many plans, it seems. Plans woven together like a net, so that if we are not caught one way, we will be caught another." Lief stared at the surface of the river, that smooth, gliding surface below which horrors drifted and squirmed.

"The Shadow Lord may have plans," said Barda quietly. "But this time, they have failed. And why? Because he made an error. He did not count on the pirates. They blundered in and tore his net to shreds."

"And if we are fortunate, he will not find out, at least for a while. For who is there left to tell him?" Jasmine added. She glanced at Lief and Barda. "So does this mean that, for now, we can stay together?"

Lief put his fingers over the Belt of Deltora, now hidden under his shirt once more. He traced the shapes of the six gems in turn, and knew the answer. "We must stay together," he said. "Like the gems in the Belt, we need one another. For faith. For happiness. For hope. For luck. For honor. And for truth."

Barda nodded firmly.

They clasped hands briefly, then lay back to rest. Another long, perilous journey lay ahead of them — a journey to the place called the Valley of the Lost. The great diamond, symbol of purity and strength, the seventh and last stone of the Belt of Deltora, was waiting for them there.

Now all they had to do was find it.